TIME PIECE

A TIME TRAVEL CRIME THRILLER

A NOVEL BY

PETER SAO-LEVENE

Table of Contents

TIME PIECE

Chapter 1.

The gavel hit the auctioneer's desk with a loud bang.

"Sold, two thousand six hundred and twenty pounds! Thank you Mr. Campbell, I'm sure Mrs. Campbell will like that piece! " Smiling, Mr. Campbell a thin older man wearing glasses, gave a nod and mouthed 'she will' silently in agreement.

"Our next item in the catalogue is number 42, very nice this time piece, a Chippendale style Mahogany Grandmother clock. Dated 1900. From a good maker and a lot of interest shown. We have several commissioned bids and there are also overseas and intercounty buyers on the net."

Let's start the bidding at three thousand five hundred pounds on commission, four thousand internet, four thousand five hundred commission, five thousand internet. Commission bids are out. At five thousand pounds internet, five thousand five hundred in the room, six thousand internet." There was brief pause. "Are we still in sir?" He said looking at the bidder in the audience.

"It's still with the net."

"Just look at that wonderful fret work and the gothic influenced carving to the frieze and door. There's a brass arch dialed three train clock movement, chiming on the hour and half hour.

"Six thousand five hundred thank you sir. Internet, are **you** still with us?

"I'll take a hundred pounds if you like. One hundred we have, six thousand seven hundred back in the room, six eight internet. One more sir? Okay then Six thousand eight hundred and fifty. The internet is out. Six thousand eight hundred and fifty pounds - any more bids? Six thousand eight hundred and fifty pounds going once. Going twice. Are we all finished?"

BANG

"Sold to buyer 179 for six thousand eight hundred and fifty pounds."

"Item number 43. Let's have a look, ah yes the blue vase."

Luigi turned and looked at me, a big smile on his face. "Here we go Joe. Hey that rhymes" he giggled in an awkwardly childish way, especially for such a hard-nosed gorilla type. "Here we go – Joe"

I tentatively smiled back and returned my focus to the auctioneer.

"Listed as circa 50 a.d. – although no exact date has been ascertained, is this blue Imperial Roman cameo glass vase.

"There's not a scratch on this vase. A1 condition?

Mmmh. Oh well that's what we've been told and that's what we are selling. I'm sure you've all had a look at it. What shall we start with, twenty thousand pounds?"

Luigi gave me a nudge and rubbed his hands together.

"You could own your very own Portland vase here, only yours will be in perfect condition. Very rare items like this should be selling at least 10 times this amount.

Who'll give me a start – five thousand pounds," Nobody stirred.

"Three thousand. Anyone?" Silence

"Ok we'll pass that one in. Take it away Frank." The auctioneer shook his head, uttering something indiscernible as the porter took the vase away.

Luigi stood up and looked angrily at me.

"The boss ain't gonna be a 'appy with this Joe." His broad Italian accent seemed to intensify with his anger. "We'd better get back to the house and report to Mr. Infanta, 'Carlos' he called out, speaking to another Infanta henchman, who'd been standing just behind us at the back of the auction room. "Go pick up the vase, we'll take it back with us."

"We might have to wait till the auction is finished to pick it up Luigi" I told him.

"Ok - Carlos, you go wait for the vase. Bring it back to the house as soon as you get it. You Joe," There was a pregnant pause. "You, come with me!"

The drive back to the house was slow. London traffic was heavy all of the time, but the M4 and the M25 were particularly bad that late evening, and this trip was made to feel even longer by the sheer silence in the car. The tension was making me feel more than a little uneasy. It had been raining lightly and the whole atmosphere was negative.

Arriving at the Infanta property approximately one and a half hours later, the huge cast iron gates providing entry past the twelve foot high, razor wire topped wall that surround the house and grounds, opened automatically. Luigi still had an air of disappointment and anger. There was a further 160 metres driveway ahead after the gates, but I already realized that it was too late to try and do a runner, even if I could.

Lorenzo Infanta's 'house' was an imposing 12 bedroom Georgian style manor nestled in amongst other well-to-do properties close to Virginia Water. Although a new build, being only about 3 years old, it was a very fitting dwelling for a wealthy Italian 'businessman' of Mr. Infanta's status within the not so legal market he dealt with.

One of the two doormen opened the front door as we reached the top step.

Luigi signaled for me to stay in the hallway as he tapped on the drawing room door and not waiting for a reply he went straight in, closing the door behind him.

After waiting only a couple of minutes, the door opened and Danny, who looked a little like a young Danny Kaye with muscles and a broken nose, beckoned me to come in.

Mr. Infanta was sitting in his usual seat, wearing his usual evening coat and holding a glass of his usual port.

"Luigi, Luigi, Luigi. How many times do I have to tell you, Dr. Bedford is not my normal type of business erh - acquaintance." He looked over to where I was standing and indicated that I should sit opposite him. "Dr. Bedford is a special partner in this new venture of ours and as a good friend of Miss Samantha's, he is our guest. We must put faith in him. Don't you be overly concerned about the vase not selling, I'm positive Dr. Bedford can clear matters up. Heh Joe, what went wrong at the salesroom?"

I sat down as Danny brought me a large cognac, placing it on the coffee table in front of me.

Nodding my thanks to Danny and looking Lorenzo Infanta straight in the eye to try to seem as confident as I could, I then replied; "It's as I said Mr. Infanta. This was only a trial run. I sensed the auctioneer didn't have belief in the authenticity of the vase. That no doubt told on the potential buyers at the auction. With the vase in an almost new like condition and no provenance as to why a 1900 year old vase should be in such excellent condition, people must have thought it a fake."

There was another knock on the door, Carlos walked straight in carrying the vase. Without saying anything, he placed it on the table and with a light bow to Mr. Infanta, walked straight out again closing the door behind him.

Both Carlos and Danny I figured to be about 30yrs old. Carlos of Italian background like most of Mr. Infanta's staff, Danny had a pure cockney accent.

Both looked like they would be able to handle themselves in a fight!

Mr. Infanta rose from his seat placing his glass on the coffee table nestled between us and walked towards the vase.

Picking it up, he gazed at the intricate detail of ancient Roman life that it depicted. A look of sheer admiration could be seen on his aged Italian face. "Not a problem Joe, not a problem at all." He placed the vase back down in the exact centre of the table, turning it slightly to rest in the perfect position. "And how elegant she looks sitting here in my drawing room. Every man needs a little trinket or two for themselves. I'm a keeping this one anyway."

I tried not to let my relief show too much.

"Mr. Infanta, we need a strategy so that with the next item we *collect*, a similar thing doesn't happen. How would you feel if I retired to my room now and put my mind to work at finding a solution?"

"Good idea Joe. Let's say we meet up at breakfast, 7.30 sharp. You can tell me your plans then."

I thanked him, stood up, made the customary bow and walked towards the door passing Luigi who stood between myself and the exit.

Luigi was a few years older than the other two, maybe early forties? Also like Danny, he sported a broken nose that didn't quite match the fine bespoke suit he wore, Luigi must have weighed half as much again than my own 203lbs. And I got the distinct impression that he was disappointed that he wasn't going to solve this problem by his regular methods.

"7.30 sharp it is. See you then." I said looking Luigi in the face as I walked past him.

Back in my room, rather than thinking about the aging of our acquired items, my mind was more intent on thoughts of how I'd managed to get into this predicament in the first place.

The memories took me back 2 years to when as a 26yr old, I started working as a Reader in Quantum Physics with the Cavendish Laboratory, at the Ray Dolby Centre in West Cambridge. My own private work had led me to discovering a way to travel back in time. Yes, you read that correctly, as hard as it may be to believe, I invented time travelling equipment!

Back then my thoughts were for only using this new found capability for doing good. With current day issues of the world being over populated, insufficient water and food, escalating sickness and violence and the inequity of wealth distribution to name a few, the entire globe was in a real mess.

What had I been able to do to alleviate any of these issues? – nothing at all!

The main road block was not being able to travel forward in time. The pattern of any future timeline just didn't exist yet. Movement in time could only happen into the past, a timeline that had already been established.

Fortunately travel back to the present was fine because that timeline was already set.

It meant that any one going back in time could move forward in time again to any point up to the very nanosecond they had gone back from, but not any further.

Without being able to go forward to the future, I wasn't able to access developments in medicine or food production that surely would be made.

It was at this stage I'd met and fallen madly in love with the new Visual Arts graduate, Sam. Samantha Infanta that is! I know what you're thinking, Lorenzo Infanta's daughter, but no; Sam was Mr. Infanta's *niece*.

She had lived with her uncle for the last ten years after Lorenzo's brother Massimo - Sam's father, had been killed in a terrible car accident in Italy. Sam's mother had been in the car at the same time but had been thrown from the car before it had hurtled over a cliff. She was in a coma and still being kept alive by life support in a hospital in Napoli.

Sam and her siblings were currently visiting their mother at the hospital.

Anyway, I digress. Sam was in Italy and that was probably for the better. I missed her terribly, but who knew what dangers these latest developments would bring.

Under the prompting of Mr. Infanta, I had travelled back in time to Pompeii, 78 A.D. with Carlos to 'help out'. Smells and sights were very different back then. A few children running here and there, some playing with hoops and sticks, some pretending to be soldiers engaged in mock sword fighting. One young child, maybe 6 or 7 years old was slumped against a wall looking very yellow and sick, almost at death's door I'd say.

It was extremely hard not to stop and help him and indeed numerous adults were looking in a similar condition. Was it Yellow Fever or something even more sinister? No, best to stay clear!

I was surprised to see very few actual beggars, most of that part of town area we were in was quite affluent looking and the one beggar that we did catch sight of was caught with a strong back hander from a man dressed in military garb which sent him flying through the dust and debris into a side street.

As hard as it was to not stop and help some of these unfortunates, we had to press on. It was enough for me to keep Carlos focused on the task at hand with all the attention we were getting from some of the women and there was graffiti in many places depicting some very lewd scenes, all of it not quite what I had expected to find!

We needed to locate a merchant who sold top class items, buy what we could with the fake gold coins we had and get out before further risk of changing the timeline in a drastic way.

Mr. Infanta's 'costume department', Graham and Milly Higgins, had rigged us up with the right style clothing. I wore a tunic and sandals as if a wealthy merchant from a far off land. Carlos wore similar garb but looked more like that of a trusted right hand man. Both of us also wore sheathed short and medium sized daggers. These were more of a deterrent from would be thieves rather than weapons we were going to actually use.

Mr. Infanta's forgers had done an epic job on the coins. It was just the language we had difficulty with. Latin, Greek and some Hebrew were supposedly in common use just before Mount Vesuvius erupted, but many were speaking something totally unrecognizable, which I later was told could have been 'Oscan'.

No, I'd never heard of it before either. Still, our far off origins act helped people to see why we might struggle with the language.

Before long we had located an upmarket stall which extended some 30 or 40 metres into a building. The items at the front weren't what we were looking for, but with there being several guards in place we were hopeful of something more precious inside and we weren't disappointed.

The aforementioned vase at the auction was positioned on a central table, together with various gold and silver items - plates, goblets, animal figures and the like. The vase rested on its own pedestal, standing proudly to catch the eye of all potential purchasers.

The shop keeper was a very hard bargaining man. If I hadn't known our gold coins to be fake, I'd have felt that *we* had been ripped off! After we'd finally agreed to a price of 12 coins, Carlos gently put the vase into a hessian simple style bag that had been slung over his shoulder and which also contained two of the four time travel units. The other two units I carried in a similar bag.

Then a disturbance outside drew everyone's attention to the front of the store. As it was passing by, I decided that that should be the limit of our initial trip back in time and took the opportunity to quickly set up the time travelling equipment in a quiet corner of the store while the store owner and guards were rubber necking towards the commotion.

With restrictions in being able to influence the people more than I already had, I wasn't feeling totally comfortable at leaving without being able to warn the locals to get as far away from Pompeii as possible before the volcano erupted. But to purposely change the timeline in such a way was something strictly against the rules.

Ok it was self-imposed rules, but if anyone now survived who had previously perished, the whole past 2,000 years of history risked drastically being changed and I had no way of knowing at this stage whether we would return to our own timeline or some timeline very different to what we knew!

Reluctantly we returned to the point we had left from in the right timeline, leaving those in Pompeii to their fate.

Now back in Mr. Infanta's Virginia Water home June 2025, things were not going entirely to plan.

Mr. Infanta had assured me that collecting precious items from the past that no longer existed or were listed as 'missing, whereabouts unknown', could raise much needed funds that would be used to help thousands of needy people.

Alright I hear you and yes, I am gullible, very gullible indeed!

I was taken in hook, line and sinker, at first.

Now I realized that the only person who was going to benefit from any wealth gain was Lorenzo Infanta himself.

The problem now was to try to get out of this sticky situation while trying to keep my relationship with Sam intact. Oh and also try and stay alive, just a minor side issue! Luigi already had me in his sights. Almost measuring me up with his eyes for the size hole that would be required to dig in order to bury my 6'1" body!

To give me more time to come up with such solutions, I needed to play along for a short while, perhaps even find a temporary answer to the authenticity problem. Yes, I would keep up Mr. Infanta's little game until a complete and safe exit became available.

Could we hide any of the items we acquired on future expeditions somewhere they would be safe and still be able to age appropriately?

What about collecting items that had *more recently* gone missing or been destroyed. Could we dream up some story that could explain transfer of ownership to Mr. Infanta?

Ironic isn't it. Here I am the inventor of time travel and for me personally, well time I felt was beginning to run very short!

I was getting tired. Sam was going to call me at 6.30 U.K. time the next morning. I had some ideas, but for now its sleep.

Chapter 2.

After a fitful night, I got up extra early and went for a run, joined of course by the ever present Carlos. "For your own safety," Mr. Infanta had told me. I doubted that very much. More like so that I didn't run off and leave him without this latest opportunity to increase his ill-gotten gains.

I tried to get to know Carlos better while running. He told me he had come from a poor family which had been living in the suburbs of Milan. He had spent some time in prison for petty crimes, mainly stealing in order to help feed his mother and two younger siblings, their Spanish father having deserted them years previously.

Mr. Infanta had hired him only a few months ago and brought him to England after helping him escape further prison time when charged with another minor incident. Carlos felt that Mr. Infanta had paid the police to drop the charges, but wasn't too sure! I immediately realized that Infanta was using that 'purchase' as a hold on Carlos. It was hard to assess how loyal to Infanta he was.

One thing that gave me a small amount of hope and pleasure, was that Carlos was no-where near as fit as I was. When push came to shove, I'd be at least able to easily outpace him. But of course not outrun his bullets!

When showered and dressed for the day ahead, I went to the lounge to receive Sam's call.

Mr. Infanta was already using the house phone speaking in Italian.

Since the reception inside the house was poor and going outside to use my mobile could arouse some suspicion, I had to wait for him to finish.

Dressed in an Italian suit that cost more than a small car, I knew Mr. Infanta was going 'on business' today. 69, maybe 70 years old but looking every bit like a man in total control of all that came his way, Lorenzo Infanta appeared the quintessential mafia style boss. He even had the look of Marlon Brando about him!

"Non ti preuccupare, Giorgio. So che è difficile. Ma cos'altro possiamo fare? Fatti coraggioso, ora devo andare. Comunque dare tutto il mio amore alla famiglia. Ciao"

"(Don't stress Giorgio. I know it's hard, but what else can we do, be brave. I have to go now, anyway give my love to all the family. Ciao")

He replaced the old fashioned 1990's style handset and turned to me.

"Ah Joe, good morning my boy. I'm so sorry," he continued, "Samantha cannot speak with you this morning. She is - how you say, 'troppo sconvolto', too upset. Her dear mama has taken a decidedly bad turn for the worse."

Mr. Infanta's face screwed up in an attempt to look grieved.

Sorry, maybe it was genuine feelings for his sister-in-law's plight. I shouldn't be negative all the time concerning Mr. Infanta.

"The doctors fear it is now time to turn off the machines and let, let nature take its course. Giorgio and the younger brothers are taking good care of Sam, so do not worry, she will be fine in time."

Carlos, who had crept in behind me, cleaned up but still showing signs of recovering from the run, walked over to where Mr. Infanta was sitting, bending down, he whispered something to him.

Mr. Infanta looked at Carlos. I could tell he wasn't that happy! *"Ok Carlos. Ma ricordati quello che ti ho detto l'ultima volta. Nienti errori quest volta!"*

("Ok Carlos, but remember what I told you last time. NO slip ups with this one").

"Get Luigi to come in here and you be back before we have to leave. Go".

Carlos bowed and quickly left the room.

"Joe we have to have our little planned business talk now, something has come up for later this morning that I need to prepare for. I hope you don't mind?"

"Not at all Mr. Infanta." As if I really had a choice in the matter.

"Ah Luigi, you're here. Come both of you sit over there." He pointed to our designated couch. The look on Luigi's face told it all. First a second of pure terror, followed quickly by a look that said 'Wow, I've just been promoted and won the lottery at the same time.' It was the first time he'd been allowed to sit in Mr. Infanta's presence. Maybe the old man was going soft in his old age!

"Mr. Infanta," I started the conversation, "as I said last night, we need to be able to age the items somehow. Perhaps we could hide them in a certain place that we know will not be disturbed for years.

"My Family has a property near Turin that's been locked up for over 30yrs." Luigi chimed in. "we could take them there, hide them in say 1995 and go to retrieve them when we get back to this time."

"Luigi, you have some brains in that head of yours after all. That's not such a bad idea. You positive that not one person has accessed the property in all that time?"

"Positive Mr. Infanta, it's my parent's property, my brother lives a mile up the road on the same estate. He farms the property around the old house and no-one ever goes there anymore, they feel it would be unlucky to go inside." Luigi answered.

"We would probably have to repeat the process several times, moving the item each occasion to a slightly different position. With careful planning, we could age an item many years in just one day!" I added

"Beautiful, that's one way we do things." Mr. Infanta agreed. "Another is that I have a certain friend, a Sergei Kolinsky who has some people who might be able to skillfully age some of the items. I will call him when I return later this evening."

"Mr. Infanta please, it's very important remember that we don't involve too many people with how we are able to obtain the items. We don't want the time travel apparatus to fall into the wrong hands. It could be very dangerous, we would have police, military, secret service and who knows what others trying desperately to get their hands on them." I didn't mention other 'crime gangs!'

"Of course Joe don't you worry, I will tell Sergei that my people have reproduced the items and to help an old friend with some extra income, I am allowing his people to work on the project for a handsome share of the sale value. How does that sound?"

"Yes, good Mr. Infanta. If your friend agrees and no-one else gets wind of the actual collection method, I think that will work."

"Fine." Mr. Infanta stood up which made Luigi also jump up and stand to attention, the 'honeymoon' period seemingly over.

"Joe, you go and get yourself something for breakfast. Mrs. Badgley is working in the kitchen today, she will take good care of you. And after that, start thinking of which items we will acquire next. Luigi and I have some vital matter to attend to alone. I will see you at dinner time after I've spoken to Sergei."

I walked through to the dining room, Mrs. Badgley came in from the kitchen at the same time with a tray of cutlery which she placed on a nice period dresser.

Now there was one sour looking old lady if ever I saw one. Early to mid-seventies I guessed and walking with a slight limp, the expression on her face told that the whole world was against her.

"Good morning Mrs. Badgley," I said cheerfully. "Mr. Infanta said you'd be able to get me some breakfast - how about a toasted bacon and egg sandwich, please?"

She nodded approval without a word and returned to the kitchen.

The dining room was furnished just as the rest of the house, impeccably. Why someone would desire even more material wealth was beyond my own desire or understanding. But as I mentioned before, this world is full of imbalance, the have's few in number. The have not's – into the billions!

Mrs. Badgley came in with a tray of coffee and cream and placed it on the table, leaving the room again without saying a word. A lot of quiet people around this place, maybe Mr. Infanta had had their tongues cut out!

I shivered at the thought. It wasn't beyond the realms of all possibility that's exactly what could happen!

I picked up a note pad and pen from the top of the dresser and sat down and poured some coffee. The coffee was excellent, at least if I was going to die, my last days would be lived in absolute luxury.

Noting down sources of information, I then started to think about what the next targeted pieces were going to be, their locations in place and time and the situation that caused them to become 'lost' treasures. It was important that known treasures in current existence be eliminated from the list. Any change in the known time line could have drastic effect on today's world as I have already mentioned.

My sparse knowledge of the subject of 'lost works of art' was insufficient to come up with any firm ideas on actual items we could aim for. One of my friends from Cambridge that graduated the same year that I had and now worked as Assistant Professor of the History of Medieval Art at the National Museum would know exactly the sort of things we were looking for, but I didn't want to keep adding to the list of people in on the act. Again the less people that know about the time travelling, the better. Besides I wouldn't want any friends to risk being tied up with Infanta's criminal affairs and that meant, of course, not getting Sam involved.

I needed to search the internet, maybe even the library at Cambridge, or the National Art Library.

And because of the language issues on the Pompeii trip, maybe somewhere more local and recent would be better.

Mrs. Badgley came in with breakfast, I put the pen down.

"Thank you Mrs. Badgley, that looks delicious. Have you had breakfast yourself?" I asked.

She just stood there, silent with the same sour look.

Then, all of a sudden her whole demeanor softened. She slunk to the chair next to mine, her face full of concern. She quickly looked around to the two entrance doors that lead into the dining room, placing both her hands on my forearm closest to her.

"Dr. Joe, you seem like a very nice man." She looked around again. "I must warn you. Get out of here as soon as possible. There is danger! Mr. Infanta is not the man you may think he is. He uses people to get whatever he can and then…" She moved her hand across the front of her neck, leaving me in no doubt what she meant.

"My husband, his name is also Joe. He is serving 18 years in Strangeways Prison for a double murder that he never committed. He was a stool pigeon for Infanta's top man Tommaso."

"You mean 'fall guy', he took the blame for the man Tommaso, at Mr. Infanta' orders."

"Yes, but under threat of death to our grandchildren living near Manchester. If he knew I am telling you this, he would kill us all."

"Your grandchildren and their parents, are they safe now, at this moment?" I asked.

"Our son Stephen works as a computer programmer. Sharon his wife looks after the three grandchildren at their home near Altrincham. They are good children Dr. Joe, very bright. They deserve to live a full life. Please help us." Tears dropped from one side of Mrs. Badgley's face.

"What about Tommaso, where is he now?"

"Mr. Infanta, he sent Tommaso to Italy to head his business over there and to keep him out of sight of the local police. Now, Marco is Mr. Infanta's right hand man here in England."

"Mrs. Badgley," I took hold of her hand and assured her, "I definitely won't say a word to anyone, but I will promise to do everything in my power to try to get us out of this. Try and go about your usual duties normally. I need time to think, to plan."

Mrs. Badgley composed herself, drying both eyes with a tissue. Then standing up she put the sour look back on her face, thanked me and returned to the kitchen.

I no longer felt hungry. Things had just become very much more urgent. Leaving the table and bacon and egg sandwich behind, I headed for my room.

The first thing I did was to message Sam. Not mentioning any of the issues here in England in case my phone was being monitored, I just encouraged her, expressing my love and explaining that her uncle had told me what was happening in Napoli and that I hoped to be there with her in Italy soon.

While still reflecting on Sam, I recalled a time we had spent together when we had just started seeing each other.

We had lunched at the Riverside Café on Lambeth Pier and then decided to walk off the meal on a local tour of some of the Westminster buildings.

The tour had taken us to a few places such as Lambeth Palace, Westminster Bridge, the Royal Air

Force Memorial on Victoria Embankment and to the Banquet house and gardens of the old Whitehall Palace.

Whitehall Palace itself had been the home of some of the past English royals.

The last to reside there was William the third and Queen Mary. They had not been in residence in the first week of January 1698 when it was totally destroyed by fire, along with many of its treasures. The only building left standing - the tour guide had said, was the Banquet House. That could serve as a location point for the time travelling, a space common in both time periods would use less power and presented less risk of being transported into something solid.

After a little internet research, I was able to ascertain that destroyed in that fire, were some famous works of art, notably Hans Holbein the Younger's "Portrait of Henry VIII" and Gian-Lorenzo Bernini's marble portrait bust of Charles 1'

This was our next target location, January 1 1698, Whitehall Palace!

Chapter 3.

The planning for the Whitehall trip went as expected.

We needed costumes and some refreshers on Elizabethan English. Also we decided to take some more gold coins in case we needed them, not necessarily for purchases, but rather to offer as bribes.

The royals I had learnt, had hardly been visiting the palace for years, they preferred other royal residences. Consequently only a skeleton staff was known to be in residence at the time of the fire. Planning the time of our trip for the wee hours of the morning and being in the very chilly English winter, those staff would most likely be well tucked up in bed.

Still in case we did meet up with any guards etc., we rehearsed stories of what we were doing there. I was going as an army captain with orders to retrieve some items for moving to Windsor. We had documents of procurement to legitimize our removal of specific items. Sergei's team had been able to forge the king's ring seal which added a truly authentic touch to the documents.

Carlos was going as a king's guard and under strict instructions to play dumb as his accent would have been very hard to explain.

Mr. Infanta had wanted more of his men to go, but as I explained, the time travel equipment's capacity over a 350 year trip was limited to just the two of us and what we had targeted to bring back. I had been working over the past year to increase the power of the time travel units, but as yet had not succeeded.

I tried talking with the Higgins' while they were fitting me out with my latest costume. Of course I needed to be discreet in order not to arouse suspicion.

"You guys are extremely good at these costumes." I complimented Graham and Milly. "You're obviously top theatre costume makers."

"Thank you, replied Graham, "we've done our fair share with the Royal Shakespeare in the past."

"And now you're working for Mr. Infanta! A bit of a waste of your talents with this limited work perhaps?" I enquired.

Graham and Milly looked at each other. They were two peas from the same pod – wiry and prematurely aged. "Mr. Infanta pays very well", Milly said.

"We do all of his own clothes and also some of Mr. Infanta's staff and friends, like we're doing this for you and Carlos."

Milly's 'matter of fact' tone told me not to push it any further. It was clear to me that Infanta had a hold on this poor couple as well!

I decided there and then not to enquire with any other of Mr. Infanta's staff as a precaution, not wanting to alert him to any idea that I wanted out. Mrs. Badgley had approached me so that was different. Then a thought struck me. What if Infanta had put Mrs. Badgley up to it? I shivered. There's no doubt that I needed to be much more careful until I knew who I could really trust and who I couldn't!

Then I thought of Sam. No, she was the one person whom I could totally trust. I shook the thought from my mind immediately.

We'd only known each other seriously for about 4 months, but she'd be horrified to find out that Uncle Lorenzo wasn't the sweet, nice, caring relative she thought he was.

After being fitted out with the 1690's gear, the Higgins' left to finish off some last minute alterations.

Now my focus was turned to the actual time travelling element of the trip.

When developing the time travelling equipment, I'd put much thought into the 'mode' that I would use.

However the power issue and actual nature of time itself, dictated the mode somewhat, so no bracelets, no chairs with spinning wheels behind them or capsule like pods could be used. Being restricted as such meant designing four floor lamp-like devises that stood about three foot tall. One was the control unit that worked as a quantum transmitter. The other three units received and reflected the 'wave particle duality' emissions around the enclosed area created by the placement of the four units.

The effect was like throwing a stone into pond water. As the ripples extend outwards they reach the point of hitting an embankment or wall. At that point they are reflected and start moving backwards along the same path they had originally come from, but using my set up, with increased energy.

The result with the time travelling units being that everything within the containment field created by the four units, including the units themselves could be moved to any preprogrammed position in time and/or space.

Power usage was governed by the mass within the field, the distance – both space and time needing to be travelled and the perimeter size of the field itself.

Therefore if the space distance was reduced, the more power was available for increasing the mass and time distance.

That meant that if we could actually start from within the Palace compound, we would have sufficient power to bring more and/or heavier items back with us.

That night at dinner Mr. Infanta seemed more than a little rattled. Luigi was nowhere to be seen. Carlos and the previously unseen Marco had been huddled at the far end of the dining room conversing in hushed secrecy. Often Marco, a man of about 45 years old with a scar down one side of his face, would glance up at me, then to Mr. Infanta and then back to the conversation with Carlos.

Mr. Infanta spoke only a few words to agree with whatever I had mentioned as to how the plans were going. He said he'd come to a full agreement with his friend Sergei and that Sergei didn't doubt Mr. Infanta's explanation of where the items originated. However Mr. Infanta was a troubled man. To say he was preoccupied would be a gross understatement. Gone was the self- assured 'Boss' man who had been in full control. I doubted whether he had really heard anything that I had said to him.

Whatever had transpired during the day had put all of them on edge and that in turn made me more nervous than I had been previously.

Deciding not to interfere, their problems were their problems. I had enough of my own to sort out.

Mr. Infanta and the other two retired to the study, leaving most of their meals untouched.

Unlike most of the downstairs facilities, the study is one place I hadn't been allowed inside.

"This Joe, is my personnel business space. Totally out of bounds to anyone I haven't specifically invited. *Ai capito*" ("Understand!") Mr. Infanta had directed me in no uncertain terms when I'd first been invited to stay at the house, now about twelve days previous.

"Uncle Lorenzo, no need to bully him." Sam had said linking her arms around one of mine, coming to my protection. "Joe has no reason to go into that stuffy old study room. Besides he'll be spending all his time paying attention to me." She added, flickering her eyes in mock innocence.

Next she smiled a smile that would have melted the coldest of hearts, it certainly did mine at the time.

The memory brought a warm smile to my own lips as I reflected on how I'd fallen more deeply in love with Sam at that very moment.

I looked up at Mrs. Badgley who had entered the dining room to clear away the dishes.

Looking directly into my eyes she fearfully mumbled, "Better sort those escape plans out pretty quickly Dr. Joe. I think time maybe running out!"

She returned to the kitchen leaving the table partly uncleared.

Retiring to my room to put in the finishing touches in preparation for tomorrows trip to the past, I also started to put in some serious thoughts of how to end my involvement in Mr. Infanta's scheming games.

After the trip back to the late 1600's, I needed to meet up with Sam in Italy to be by her side at her moment of need, if Mr. Infanta didn't like that, then tough. My adrenaline was getting into full swing and it was time I took control of my own future!

I felt defiant and strong. I had to be if I was going to survive this.

But I also needed to make sure that what I put into place was going to work, for Mrs. Badgley, Sam's and my own sake.

"Play it cool Dr. Joe, play it cool" I told myself, mimicking how Mrs. Badgley addressed me.

I sent a text to Sam expressing my love for her and my hope that we'd soon be together.

Next I checked the fake letter from 'King William' plus the coins. I then reviewed some phrases to mention if we were to meet up with anyone at the Palace.

Then time was spent to finish prepping the equipment. Adjusting the settings for the correct location and time and leaving the ancillary units on charge overnight.

The main unit of the four had its own power pack that I'd designed and built myself. I didn't have any spare power pack or recharge capability for that unit with me. The only method of powering that one back up lay safely locked away in my rooms at The

Cavendish Laboratory. The digital display told me there was 51% charge left. Plenty of power for the required journey and the expected mass to be transported back to the current time and location.

I looked at my watch. 10.25 p.m. The Higgins would be back here at the house in about eleven hours with the costumes.

Setting my alarm for 6.00, I turned off my phone and placed it on the bedside table.

Tomorrow was going to be a very long day!

Chapter 4.

Both Carlos and I appeared simultaneously in the banquet hall of 1698, it was dark and bitterly cold.

Hiding the time travel equipment behind a large wall tapestry, we exited the banquet hall in the westerly direction towards the main palace building.

The night sky was clear and surprisingly bright, the moon doing a wonderful job even through the mist that was starting to form.

It took us all of 15 minutes to locate the Portrait of Henry VIII. The surrounding frame was huge. I tried to move it from the wall. "It's too big Carlos, it weighs too much," I whispered.

"Maybe we cut it out from the frame and roll it." Carlos suggested. "It's going to burn anyway if we leave it."

Without waiting for my answer, he pulled out a knife and jumped up onto the cabinet resting underneath the portrait.

Cutting as close to the inside of the frame as possible, he quickly started moving the knife through this priceless canvass.

"Shhh. Can't you cut any quieter?" I said, again in a whisper as I looked around for anyone who might have heard us.

"I could, but if I take any longer in cutting it out, we'll either get caught or I'll freeze to death!" Carlos replied a little sarcastically. "Does your time machine gizmo have any issues working in these conditions?" he asked.

"Shouldn't be a problem, never tested it." I said as if there may be some doubt. Still looking around, I knew there definitely wouldn't be an issue, it may even work better in the cold. I just wanted to put the wind up Carlos a bit. It helped me feel more in control of my situation.

Carlos finished cutting the portrait and rolling it up. After he jumped down with a little more grace than I would have believed him capable of, we headed back towards the last junction in the palace corridors we had passed. Enroute we removed several other smaller, less massive paintings, this time with their frames.

"Let's get these back to the banquet hall and then return to look for the King Charles bust down that other corridor." Carlos suggested.

"We don't want to stay here anymore than absolutely necessary." I replied. "It increases the opportunity of being caught."

"We got back up plans haven't we? What are they for if not to be used!"

"There's no point in pushing our luck Carlos. We're not invisible or invincible. We could get injured, killed or even taken captive to spend the rest of our miserable lives in the Tower dungeons. How do you fancy that?"

Carlos looked undeterred. "You worry too much doc. I tell you what. You stay with the goods in the banquet hall, setting up the time travel gizmo. I'll go back for the bust. I know what it looks like from the pics we studied. I'll be back before you know it."

"OK Carlos." I conceded. "But I don't like it. And I want you to cancel all ideas of the bust and hightail it back to me the first inkling of trouble. Got it?"

"Fine doc, but it's gonna be all good, you'll see"

As soon as we arrived back at the banquet hall, Carlos left the things he was carrying and disappeared back outside.

After watching him go, I made haste in setting up the time travel units with the return coordinates and placing the paintings we had collected in one corner of the travel field and myself in another corner closest to the control unit, leaving enough room for Carlos and the bust. Then I waited.

The minutes seemed to slow dramatically. I checked through the window to try and see Carlos, nothing.

Spending another few seconds re-checking the positioning and the settings for the return trip directly back to the Infanta mansion co-ordinates, it seemed like too much time had elapsed. I looked anxiously towards the door Carlos had exited from.

Suddenly there was shouting from outside. Carlos burst in through the door, struggling with the bust.

It was obvious that we'd also underestimated the weight of the bust. Gasping, Carlos deposited it in one of the free corners of the travel field and positioned himself in the last remaining spot. "Go, go, go." He shouted.

"Carlos, there's too much weight we won't make it back. Take the bust out and let's go."

The shouting, although still indiscernible, was getting much closer.

"No." Carlos yelled jumping out of the area of the travel field. "Take the bust and come straight back for me. The boss will be angry if we don't get it to him first up. Set the timer thingy for one second after you leave this time for when you return and come back for me. It'll be ok doc. Go please."

I pressed the switch on the control unit just as the door flew open and a very rough looking Captain of the Guards stormed in followed by at least one other guard, both with swords drawn!

I looked around the room back in the Infanta mansion. I'd made it with the paintings, the Charles I bust - but no Carlos.

He was still back in 1698!

Chapter 5.

I felt guilty.

It weighed heavy on my shoulders leaving Carlos behind. Yes of course I knew that I could go back for him to 1 second past the time I'd left him.

All I thought of though, was the two iron swords coming in through the banquet hall door and the look on poor Carlos's face as he turned to view the peril he was now in.

For him though I rationalized, time in effect had stood still. I WOULD be back in time to collect him and escape the wrath of the guards. Yes I had to stay positive about it. It was the only way for me to keep a clear mind.

I took a note of the precise time of the departure from 1698 and called Luigi and Danny to pick up the treasures and take them away from me. They both arrived a couple of minutes later.

Expecting Luigi to be far from happy concerning Carlos being left behind, he strangely seemed quite pleased. Had I missed something? He didn't even interrogate me as to the circumstances leading to Carlos not returning.

"I'll look after the goods Joe. Danny go with Joe to the cellar with the time travel units, and Joe, it's best if you stayed there with your time gadgets for the moment."

Danny nodded acceptance of Luigi's command and turning to me said, "It's for the best Joe. We can't explain why, just you'll be safer down there for the time being."

Turning to pick up two of the time travel units, I decided to keep silent for the moment and not query their concerns even though I felt something serious was up. Danny picked up the other two units and led the way out towards the cellar.

Stalling just outside the door, I looked at Luigi. "Carlos will be ok, Luigi." Quickly explaining the plan to return as soon as the time travel units were back up to power I added. "And besides, Mr. Infanta will be so pleased with the things we've brought back."

"Don't worry about Carlos." He replied firmly. "Just keep your head low in the cellar Joe until we come and say it's safe to come out." Luigi then locked the door to the room with the '1698 treasures' still inside. He then hastened his retreat back towards the main hallway.

Shaking off the uncertainty, I took the remaining two time travel units to the cellar for charging.

Danny was just coming back out from the cellar as I arrived at the door.

As soon as I went in, I moved to put the units on charge when Danny tapped me on the shoulder.

"Joe. Stay here, please. As we said, it's for your own safety." He repeated what was told me upstairs. Then he turned and left the cellar, locking the door behind him.

"What!" I shouted, more to myself than to anyone who might hear me.

I ran to the door trying the door knob. Yes, locked from the outside. "Danny, let me out. You can't just lock me up in the cellar like a prisoner. What the hell is going on? Let me out." This I shouted directly to Danny, the source of my anger.

With no-one coming to my rescue, I cursed and looked around the cellar from where I was standing.

Quite spacious with lots of wine racks loaded with some very good vintage wines I'm sure.

There were a couple of fridges to one side and a nice seating area close to a small timber bar.

I put the three secondary units on charge behind the bar and opened one of the fridges. It was well stocked with various cheeses and some cold meats and a variety of condiments.

Trying the second fridge, I found mainly bottles of white wine, 2002 vintage 'Dom perignon', some Riesling, a few Italian whites, Santa Margherita Lugana and others, plus a variety of beers.

My earlier thoughts of dying in luxury came to mind when, what was that? A gun shot? And again a second almost inaudible shot confirmed that my ears hadn't deceived me.

Nervously I ran back to the door, this time making more effort to shake the door knob, trying to pull the door open. Of course it didn't budge.

Pressing my ear to the door I listened carefully for anything. No sound whatsoever coming from upstairs. I even tried the old trick of placing the open end of a tumbler glass onto the door and pressing my ear to the base of the glass in hope any sound from upstairs would be amplified. Still nothing.

Investigating the rest of the large cellar revealed no back way out. No windows either. What about the cupboards and drawers, maybe a spare key?

Searching the cupboards revealed only crockery and linen.

The top drawer contained only cutlery. The second more linen and what's that underneath the tea towels?

A hand gun!

Picking it up, I placed it straight down on top of the bar.

I've never been keen on weapons. Never even held a gun before, never mind fired one!

Was it loaded? Did it have a safety catch?

I looked towards the door, still no more sounds from upstairs.

Picking the gun up, I placed it back in the drawer under the tea towels and continued onto the last drawer. No key there either.

Sitting down on one of the seats, I suddenly realized that I was still dressed in the 1690's outfit. The two swords! Maybe I could pry the lock or door.

Back to the door, I struggled with the knife and trying to pry open the door but with no success, the blade being much too wide to fit into the lock also.

Walking over to the main time travel unit, I checked the power. About 12% left. The other units would take a while to charge enough to safely use them to escape the cellar.

Sitting back down, all I could do was to wait.

After about thirty minutes for the batteries to recharge and time enough for me to think of my next move, I set up the time travel units.

I needed to exit the cellar and be proactive in whatever was needed to solve my little problems!

Adjusting the time and space settings for my room during the time of the trip to 1698, I pressed the go switch.

Back in my room I immediately changed into some regular clothing. I had decided to bring the gun along after all, if only for moral support. Or maybe that's immoral support depending on how you look at it. I had it tucked into the back of my trousers, just as I'd seen done in the movies.

Remembering that most of the others were not home at the time we were in 1698, I moved cautiously to the kitchen to enquire if Mrs. Badgley had a key to the cellar.

She did and was happy to give it to me without question along with another key on the same keyring to a basement storeroom next to the wine cellar.

Back in my room I reset the units to return to the locked cellar a couple of seconds after I had left previously.

After unlocking the door, I placed the time travel units on charge in the other storeroom and locked both it and the cellar doors and headed up the stairs as quietly as possible.

Stopping to listen after every few steps for any signs of movement upstairs, it wasn't until I had reached the top and the hallway door that I heard anything and suddenly I froze just out of sight of those in the hallway, but with the door slightly ajar.

Mr. Infanta was saying something to one of the doormen.

I listened carefully as several sets of footsteps hurried out of the house. Three car doors opened and closed as whoever made those footsteps got into awaiting vehicles, then two car engines started and both cars were driven off at pace.

Inching ever so slightly forward to see if anyone was still in the house, I froze again with the sound of something heavy being dragged along the floor. Sneaking a peek around the corner, one of the doormen was struggling with Marco's seemingly dead body, hauling him towards the open front door by dragging him from underneath the arm pits, Marco's feet trailing along the floor and leaving some blood smudges behind.

Snapping back out of view it was time for some quick thinking.

It was impossible to try and put the pieces of the puzzle together.

With Marco dead and one doorman taking him outside, that left Infanta, Luigi, Danny and the other doorman.

Three of those had already gone in the cars, who had been left behind? Where was the other missing person, whoever they were?

I didn't have to wait long for the answers. The study door opened and Luigi came out carrying some blood stained cloths.

He dropped the cloths onto Marco's extended legs and picked up Marco's feet to help the doorman to carry him outside.

Waiting patiently and nervously, I heard them put the body into the car boot. Then someone came back inside the house while the other got into the car and started the engine.

Chancing a glimpse into the hallway, I saw Luigi cleaning up the blood stains off the hallway floor. Without him looking around, he finished that and headed straight out of the front door and into the awaiting car.

Stealing a look through the side window next to the door, I watched as the car exited through the front gates and continued down the road heading towards the M25 and London, the gates automatically closing behind them.

Walking over to the study door, I cautiously tried the handle. Unlocked! Slowly peering into the room I had been banned from, there was evidence of a struggle.

One chair lying on its side close to the open fireplace looked damaged and some papers protruding from a manila file lay on the floor.

Bending over, I carefully used a pen to open the file to examine the contents of the file without leaving any fingerprints.

A photo of Marco shaking hands with an older man I didn't recognize. Another photo, again of Marco but, this time going into a house with another man close behind him.

Were these photos anything to do with Marco being killed? It seemed obvious to me. Maybe Marco had turned traitor? Maybe the older man he was talking to was the boss of a rival crime group? I decided to take a photo of the pictures in the file and of the broken chair with my phone camera. It just felt like the best policy, maybe as some evidence for the police later?

I noticed some blood spots that hadn't yet been cleaned and took more photos of them and absorbed some of the blood onto a clean tissue which I placed in an envelope I took from the desk. Leroy Jethro Gibbs would be proud!

Enough was enough, time to leave the Infanta mansion for good. Leaving the study, I wiped the door knob of any prints and ran upstairs to pack, I wanted out!

Chapter 6.

Normally I would be very neat and tidy with my luggage packing. Not this time!

Now, I just threw everything in my bag as quickly as possible.

Checking around the room to see if everything was cleared, I picked up the bag and went down the stairs to see if Mrs. Badgley was there.

She wasn't. How could I help her to be safe without risking her and her family as well?

Choosing to write her a cryptic note which read;

Doctors surgery, phone

To make appointment for extraction

07911 654321

I gave her my second sim's number that I only normally gave to business contacts - Infanta wouldn't know it was mine, I then placed the note inside the pocket of her apron which hung on the back of the pantry door.

Hopefully she would find it and call before Infanta did something drastic to her or her family.

Leaving my bag in the pantry, I exited the back door and walked towards the garage to see if my own car was still there, it was.

Starting my burgundy coloured Pajero, I drove closer to the rear of the house. Parking close to the back door, I left the engine running and went back inside the house. There I retrieved the 4 time travel units from the storeroom in the basement, my bag from the pantry and loaded them all into the car and then drove up to the main gate.

The gate didn't open! Getting out I looked for a manual override to open the gate. Nothing! I rattled the gate - no it wasn't going to budge.

Looking up to the top of the wall, I saw the razor wire all around, as well as strategically placed security cameras, "damn!"

"What to do, what to do?" The gates were obviously too solid to ram them, no option there. Eventually someone would be looking at the footage from the cameras, too late to worry about that now.

The only thing I could do was to put the car back into the garage and use the time travel units to escape the property, the car was too massive for the amount of power I had left in the main unit, so it was back to the garage.

After unloading the units and my bag, I set the coordinates for my lab at a time I knew no one would be around and initiated the travel immediately.

Back at Cavendish Laboratory in my rooms, I put the three rechargeable units on charge and placed the main unit onto a work bench.

First I replaced the power unit with one of the spare packs I had locked up in the lab safe.

Next I needed to do some adjustments to the unit's settings program so I connected it up to my computer terminal.

The date and coordinates for each time/space trip travelled had to be programmed in manually. Thinking about going back for Carlos and any other incident where urgency in return transport was required, this method took too long. By the time I had reset the coordinates back from 1698 when I go back for Carlos as an example, the two guards would be upon us and that would be that.

I'd already been working on a 'quick dial' program, so all I had to do was to integrate it into the current set up.

Three quick dial settings were chosen, one here at the lab, one at my place near Reigate, Surrey and a third at my parent's home in Lyndhurst in the New Forest, the place I grew up.

The time settings had to have an automatic adjustment factor included. If this was set to the exact same time for every trip I used the speed dial, I could end up colliding with myself when also returning to that same time and space on a different trip.

So by programming a thirty minute additional increment to each return trip at each separate location on the speed dial, I was able to prevent some unknown drastic reaction in the time/space continuum!

And oh, if that hurts your brain, remember never to ask me about the finer details of how the time travel units work!

The settings adjustments completed, I sat back and took a deep breath. As I moved back in my chair, I felt the hand gun, still tucked into the back of my trousers.

Pulling the gun out, I stared at it in my hand for a few seconds and started to reflect again on how things had changed in my life over the last year.

I'd successfully completed my trial experiments with the time travel units. Then during a semi-private celebration of that work at the club with a few friends who thought I was celebrating a lottery win or something, well that was when I had first really noticed Sam as a potential partner in life.

Putting the gun down, I warmed at the thought of her. That moment was better than the hot shower and decent night's sleep that I so badly needed.

Deciding to research the flight schedules for Italy, Sam was slipping from being my number one concern and that had to change.

Flights around the world had almost returned back to normal after covid 19 had changed the world's outlook on international travel so much.

Prices were still way too high, but that was the least of my worries.

I confirmed a flight for 4.35p.m. in two days time and the receipt and itinerary came back immediately by email. Texting Sam the information, I expressed my love and longing to be with her.

Feeling bad about not telling her of the Whitehall Palace trip and what was happening back here in England, I ended the text by telling her I would bring her up to speed when we were together Friday night.

❖

My reflections were short lived however, suddenly brought to current realities as the vision of Marco's dead body being dragged through the front door replayed in my mind. Also Carlos and the two guards back in 1698 and Mrs. Badgley and her earnest plea for help back in the dining room.

Then a tap on the internal window stopped my thoughts and brought me back to the here and now.

"Joe, is everything alright? I thought you weren't back for another week or two. I didn't see your car in its usual space either!"

"Hello Martin." I replied, quickly moving the gun out of sight. "Yes I'm fine thanks. Oh just having car troubles and can't keep away from this place, you know how it is."

Martin who was Head of Faculty, Professor of Physics and all round nice guy, had been a solid mentor and support for me during my studies and ever since. Opening the door he came into the lab.

"You can use mine for a couple of hours if you need," He suggested jingling his keys in front of him. "You must get it back to me by ten though, I've got to pick up Lucy from Heathrow, she's back from the States visit to her folks."

I looked at my phone for the time, almost 7.55 p.m.

"Thanks Martin but I think I'll be without mine for a couple of days. I'll sort something out."

"You will insist on going with those cheap insurance companies Joe, mine gives me a replacement vehicle for the duration my car's off the road." Martin gave me his 'I've told you this a thousand times before' look. "Hey Joe, how about using a company vehicle, you're on the approved user list. I can call and book it for you if you'd like?"

"Great idea Martin, thanks. I tell you what, let me give it some thought and I'll get back to you. How does that sound?"

"No problems, anything we can do to please our star prodigy."

"Star bul…." I stopped mid-sentence and smiled at Martin. "You're a real stirrer Martin Jenkins, you know that don't you?"

Martin laughed, enjoying his usual rib at me. "That's my boy." He moved to exit the lab, "Don't let it get to you Joe. And don't forget, I'm there for you as always."

"Thanks Martin, I know. Hey please say hi to Lucy for me when you pick her up. Now get out of here and let me get some work finished."

Still smiling, he closed the door behind him and disappeared out of sight towards his own lab.

'A company vehicle!' probably a ford transit van or something similar, no thanks Martin – I've got a Bedford time machine!

Chapter 7.

Collecting my thoughts together, I put my mind on some sort of plan.

Yes Sam was number one priority and always will be. But until my trip to Naples, I needed to get things done for Mrs. Badgley and her family and try and ensure Mr. Infanta wasn't going to continually hound me to return to focusing on his needs or even worse let Luigi get to work on me for leaving the Infanta mansion in the way I had!

Where had they driven off to? Luigi and the doorman with him had probably gone to dispose of Marco's body somewhere. What about Mr. Infanta, Danny and the other doorman?

They'd left in a particular hurry, obviously something important enough for them to leave the house empty and unguarded. I suppose they were going to be back to the house eventually to get me out of the cellar and sort out the 1698 treasures. Still there was nothing I could do there for the moment.

What about Mrs. Badgley?

I needed to speak to Joe Badgley to see if he would come clean with whatever Tommaso had done and he had taken the rap for.

That meant a safe haven was needed for Mrs. Badgley and her family to keep them out of Infanta's clutches in the meanwhile. Should I go to the police? No, how could I explain the time travelling. They'd throw into the cuckoo farm and throw away the key!

"Joe Bedford" I exclaimed to myself, "Why on earth didn't you stick to plain old simple quantum physics and time travel experiments. It was a much easier life then than having to deal with all this trouble!"

I made a mental note to call Strangeways Prison to book a visit with Joe Badgley. Hopefully I could get to Mrs. Badgley come with me. I'm sure Mr. Badgley would respond more favourably with his wife's backing.

Next on the list was to locate a safe house, somewhere Mrs. Badgley and her family could stay for an unknown length of time. I had a few ideas, one being at my parents place in Lyndhurst, but I didn't know when they'd be back from their European trip. OK it would do as a temporary site for a start, until I found somewhere else.

What about my car? I had the unused power pack installed into the main time travel unit now, so let's go and get my Pajero.

I collected all four units and the gun and my bag and input the coordinates to arrive behind the garage about five minutes after I had left earlier. A quick look through the window to make sure Martin or anyone else wasn't looking and off I went. It was exactly 8.09.11p.m.

Back at the Infanta property, I furtively walked to the outside corner of the garage and chanced a look around.

As I had expected it was too soon for anyone to have returned so I went ahead with my plans.

Loading the car with all my things, I then drove as close as possible to the wall and as far away from a security camera as possible.

Climbing on top of the Pajero, I tried to peer over the wall, careful not to get myself cut to pieces with the razor wire.

The road was very quiet, Mr. Infanta had chosen his dwelling location extremely well. Fortunately there were no trees on the wall side of the road, much easier to transport the car there.

Back down from the top of the car, I positioned the time travel units and programmed the settings for just the other side of the wall with the time set for 8.09.11p.m., the exact time I had left the lab, but still within the existing time line.

Without thinking of any potential consequences, I pressed the go switch and then I was there on the road side of the wall with the car.

As soon as I arrived, a dog barked wildly at me. A young man and his dog were walking close to the spot I materialized in. If I had set the timer for just six seconds later, both the young man and the dog would have been killed.

The young man looked up, clearly oblivious as to why the dog was so upset, he being so engrossed in listening to whatever it was on his phone and had missed the whole episode, fortunately for me!

The dog was furious though. "Sorry Mr. I don't know what's gotten into him, he's usually so placid."

"No stress." I replied. "He can probably smell my cat." I lied and loaded the time travel gear into the car. I never thought I'd be glad to see someone so engrossed with their phone and missing the world around them!

Back in my car, I started the engine. That was close! I have to be more careful in the future.

Where to now? I could go back to the lab which would have more security and there were showers there also. However too many people would be asking questions as to why I was staying there.

My place near Reigate was just over thirty minutes away, but that was the most likely place Infanta would look for me.

No my parents place in Lyndhurst was best for now. They lived in a nice large period cottage on the A337 as you leave Lyndhurst to go towards Brockenhurst.

And as I previously mentioned they were away on a European trip at present, catching up on all the holidays they had missed during the Covid restrictions.

Then a brainwave hit me. They had mentioned just before they left that if I happened by their place while they were away, could I take a look over a neighbour's property nearby. That place was going to be empty until early December. That's our safe house for the Badgleys!

I knew the family who owned it well and didn't feel hesitant at all in using a place that I knew like the back of my hand from the many visits there when I was young. Of course I can't tell you exactly where it is, it is supposed to be a safe house after all!

Driving in through the gates at home brought back many pleasant memories. It was about 11p.m. by the time I arrived, having stopped at Frimley to get some food on the way.

I had lived in this house from 3 years old as an only child, right up until I started Uni. The New Forest was a fantastic place to grow up, full of mystery, wildlife and lots of adventure.

Dad would take me fishing when he could take time off work as a police detective with Hampshire police. He had retired two years previously after serving the last four yours as DCI and was now enjoying the quiet life, spending lots of time in his man cave. Those early years going fishing and boating were very precious moments, occurring too infrequently.

That left a lot of time playing with my friends, reading (science fiction of course), exploring the many exciting natural venues in and around Lyndhurst, my sporting activities and helping mum as much as I could.

I pushed those thoughts to the back of my mind, reminiscing was for another time. Funny I keep on saying that sort of thing but still tend to loose myself in my memories! I imagined I could hear Gladys Knight singing "the good old days.."

I quickly checked around the inside of the house, listened to their messages on the answerphone and then took a refreshing shower and changed into some casual clothes.

With a glass of red in hand, I did a patrol around the outside of the property. The grounds weren't extensive by any means, about one and a half acres, so I secured the gate and checked the car was safely locked up in the garage. Then I returned to the house just as my phone rang.

It was the business line, so at this time of night could be only one person, "Hello, Mrs. Badgley is that you?"

"Dr. Joe, where are you? Mr. Infanta is in a rage. They are going to kill you Dr. Joe. Oh I'm so scared."

"Mrs. Badgley, calm down, I am safe and well. What about yourself, are you safe?"

"I think so, for now Dr. Joe. When I came back to the mansion, no-one was here, I thought maybe you were hurt. Mr. Infanta eventually returned with Luigi, Danny and one of the doormen, Sebastian. They were all shaken up, like something bad happened and there's no sign of either Marco or Gian Luca."

"Gian Luca. Is that the other doorman?" I asked.

"Yes. He never goes anywhere without Mr. Infanta. I'm very worried Dr. Joe. What should I do, please help me."

Deciding not to tell Mrs. Badgley about what had happened to Marco - her nerves were already frayed enough, I told her "Mrs. Badgley calm down, I don't think that you are in immediate danger. Just keep yourself out of everyone's way and go about your duties as normally as you can. I promise that I will come and take you from there early tomorrow, do you understand?"

"But, but Dr. Joe. I am very scared, I'm not sure I can wait till morning, please."

"Everything is going to be alright Mrs. Badgley. Look its well past 11.30, just go to bed and wait for my call in the morning. I'll ring you at about 5a.m. Keep the phone close to you and try not to let anyone overhear your conversation when you speak to me. It will be fine, please believe me."

"Ok Dr. Joe, I trust you, but please don't forget me."

"I won't. You go and get some rest now, we have an early start tomorrow."

The phone connection ended abruptly. I sure hoped it was Mrs. Badgley hanging up and that no one had caught up with her!

Chapter 8.

5a.m. on the dot, I called the last incoming number on my business line, Mrs. Badgley.

She, like me hadn't slept much at all, but was very keen to exit the Infanta place.

"Dr. Joe, please get me away from here, Marco IS DEAD. They killed him, Mr. Infanta and Luigi, they shot him Dr. Joe! I heard them talking overnight."

"Mrs. Badgley, stay calm. Bring only your belongings that are most important to take and meet me at the rear of the garage, out of sight from the main house. Try not to stress, you will be safe I assure you."

Being so nervous, she dropped her phone and had to stoop to pick it back up.

I tried to calm her the best I could, but the poor woman was frantic. Definitely not the situation for the faint hearted. "I will be there waiting for you behind the garage in fifteen minutes. Trust me all will be well."

"Hurry Dr. Joe, hurry please!"

I ended the connection this time and then hastened to set up the time travel equipment - setting the speed dial for the return trip home 2 seconds after I leave for the Infanta house, the last time hopefully!

Arriving at the rear of the garage at 5.12a.m., I risked a look towards the back door. Mrs. Badgley had just opened the door and I watched as she started to walk over to the garage.

Then I felt something hard being pressed against the back of my head.

"Turn around slowly, Bedford. One false move and you die!"

I raised my hands automatically and slowly turned to face the man I now knew to be called Sebastian holding a gun and pointing it directly at my chest.

"Pretty versatile as a doorman Sebastian, it should look good on your resume."

"Wise cracking doctors though don't have much future hope Bedford, so I'd be careful who you poke fun at."

A scream diverted our attention to Mrs. Badgley who had been strong armed by Danny.

Quickly I kicked the gun from Sebastian's hand and struck him with my elbow to his chin. He went down like a lead balloon.

Turning quickly to face Danny, who had pushed Mrs. Badgley out of the way and was reaching for his gun, I jumped in axe kick mode knocking him to the ground where a '12-6' put him completely out of action.

I dragged Danny first and then Sebastian behind the garage and ushered Mrs. Badgley there also, calming her as much as I could. Oh did I forget to tell you, my sport growing up was mixed martial arts. I'm a little rusty but it still comes in useful when needed!

I did get to the National Championships at 20, but sustained an injury in warm up so had to withdraw. Pity, I was favourite to win my weight category and the World Championships beckoned afterwards. Still that's when I made a full commitment to physics and my final year of my Bachelor studies. You can't have it all!

Both Sebastian and Danny were still out cold, but would recover eventually, well maybe with more aches and pains than before!

Mrs. Badgley was sobbing and obviously very scared. "We're all right now Mrs. Badgley. Let's get you out of here.

Re-checking the time travel settings, I placed myself, Mrs. Badgley and Danny and Sebastian's guns inside the travel field and … back home.

Mrs. Badgley screamed again, only this time much louder.

"Oh Dr. Joe" she yelled at me. "What has happened?" She sobbed a few more times, rolled her eyes and fainted there and then.

Denise McIntyre, the next door neighbour had heard the scream and had come over to investigate.

She was wafting an old copy of Hare and Hounds towards Mrs. Badgley's face as she lay on the sofa where I'd moved her, the time travel equipment and the guns removed out of sight to dad's man cave before Denise came in.

Mrs. Badgley's eyes flickered open. Denise exchanged the magazine for a smelling salts sachet, which Mrs. Badgley quickly brushed away from her face and posed ready for another scream.

I moved in front of Denise so Mrs. Badgley could see me. "Mrs. Badgley it's me Joe, everything is ok you're safe now. This nice lady is Denise, she heard your scream and came to help. Don't worry we are well away from the Infanta house and Sebastian and Danny."

She sat upright, looking suspiciously at Denise. "Dr. Joe, how did, how did we get here?"

Putting my finger to my lips I said, "Shhh, you just rest up and get your breath. We can talk soon." Turning to Denise, "Denise, I'm so grateful you came to help, that's what good neighbouring is all about. I think we can manage now. A little rest and Mrs. Badgley will be fine. You'd better get back home, everyone will be wondering where you've got to."

"Are you sure Joe? I can call for a doctor if you want." She smiled, "A medical doctor that is. It would be no trouble."

"No thank you Denise, But If we need your help again, I'll be sure to let you know."

She stood up, looking at Mrs. Badgley. "You'll be fine in a few moments dearie, you just relax, I'm just next door if you need me." Denise pointed in the general direction of 'next door' and turned to exit.

"I've got to collect some fresh eggs from the girls Joe, shall I bring some around for you both?"

"That would be lovely Denise. And don't you worry either, everything will be fine."

"Mm, the most exciting start to the day we've had around here for years!" She exclaimed to herself as she exited the front door.

"Just the run of the mill kind of stuff for me these days." I muttered to myself.

Chapter 9.

After Mrs. Badgley had enjoyed the scrambled eggs I cooked with the fresh eggs Denise brought around, she began to look much better.

Over a brewed coffee, we chatted about everything as viewed from our own perspective.

She told me how the tempers had flared after Mr. Infanta had found out that I had escaped the cellar, overhearing Luigi say that he'd already shot Marco that day, so he could easily shoot me also, as soon as he got hold of me.

"Did you hear why they shot Marco?" I asked

"Yes. Marco had been found out as an undercover police agent investigating Mr. Infanta and his associates. They said that they would have to go into hiding somewhere, until they could fix the situation by pinning Marco's killing on Carlos, but with you gone they said they couldn't get hold of Carlos because he was lost back at Whitehall Palace. I'm not too sure if I remember that right, Dr. Joe. It doesn't make sense, what was Carlos doing lost in a palace?"

"It's a long story Mrs. Badgley. Carlos is safe for now, although I'm not sure why they wanted to get him in particular blamed for Marco's death. We'll sort Carlos out in due time."

We talked at length about the safe house for her and all the family.

Calling Stephen - Mrs. Badgley's son, we eventually managed to persuade him to bring his wife and the three children to the safe house. He was due some leave but they wanted to wait until Joe Badgley had agreed to tell the real story concerning Tommaso's misdemeanors.

However since I explained that now Mr. Infanta would be looking for Stephen's mother as well, now that she also had left the mansion and that put all their lives in immediate jeopardy, Stephen readily agreed to come down to the New Forest as soon as he was able to gather his wife, the children and some belongings.

Mrs. Badgley didn't like hearing that one bit and she almost broke down again at the stress of this more imminent threat to herself and family.

Managing to sooth her concerns yet again, I next focused on Joe Badgley. It so happened that Mrs. Badgley was due to visit him in prison in five days' time next Tuesday, as part of her usual scheduled visits. She'd forgotten to mention it because of all the stress.

We called Strangeways and was easily able to include myself on that same visit.

By then it was about 11.45a.m. and Mrs. Badgley, whose first name I found out was Irma, had gone for a rest. The other Badgleys wouldn't arrive into Lyndhurst until about 7.00p.m., so I sat back in my chair rubbing my hands over my face and through my hair.

This time tomorrow I would be heading out for Gatwick and my flight to see Sam in Italy. What on earth was I going to tell her?

After re-arranging my return flight for Monday so that I would be back in time to take Irma to see Mr. Badgley on Tuesday, I drove over to the safe house.

Mum had a key she kept in a kitchen draw at home, so I let myself in and scouted around, yes this place was perfect. Off the road and tucked neatly behind a dense copse of the New Forest's finest greenery, the place was just as I remembered it as a boy.

The family who lived there, the Jamiesons, had lost their son in what proved eventually to be a tragic accident when we were both about eleven years old. Dad, a Serial Sergeant back then had helped with the investigation and our two families became good friends over time. Mum had also helped with comforting them and providing as much practical assistance as she could.

Both the daughters had left home in the past few years and Mr. and Mrs. Jamieson spent much time visiting them and their new grandchildren.

I presumed that that's where they were now and probably the entire family was coming back here for the Christmas break as they did annually. Plenty of time for the Badgley's to stay for a while. I turned on the electricity and checked all was good there, leaving any housekeeping for the Badgleys which would help keep them occupied while they settled in. I then returned back to my parents place to ensure Irma hadn't woken and started panicking.

When she did finally awake about forty minutes later, we went shopping for a couple of weeks groceries, not knowing how long we would need the safe house for. Then I took Irma to the safe house to unload the shopping and to show her around.

We had also purchased a few extra mobile phones for the Badgleys and myself to use as extra security. I didn't know if Mr. Infanta had access to phone tracing technology, but for the price of a few prepaids, it wasn't worth the risk.

Spending time to activate the new sims and programming each other's new, temporary numbers into all of the new phones, we next drove to the arranged rendezvous location in Lyndhurst township after the junior Badgleys had texted Irma regarding their arrival.

From Lyndhurst with them following me, Irma had jumped into Stephen's people mover, I didn't drive directly to the safe house. Instead, wanting to know if anyone was tailing the Badgleys, we drove straight down the A337, through Brockenhurst, Boldre and into Lymington where we stopped for a while, seemingly doing the touristy activities of eating fish and chips while we looked at the boats moored there.

Satisfied that no-one was following us and getting them all to turn off their phones and give them to me for safe keeping, we finally headed for the safe house via New Milton and some back roads.

Back at the Jamieson's place after unloading the visitor's car, distributing the new mobile phones and taking all the dust sheets off the furniture, the four adults sat with some wine to talk things through while the children explored the house.

"To give everyone the best possible chance to keep safe," I started, "we have to lay down strict rules for all of us!"

"Yes we understand Joe, that's the only reason we are here in the first place. What rules do you suggest?" Sharon Badgley asked.

I wasn't yet convinced that they understood the absolute need to keep strict adherence to what I was saying. "Again Sharon, I'm sorry but I need to emphasize, these are not going to be suggestions, but MUST do's. It's the only way. Infanta and his men are ruthless and they'll stop at nothing to protect their freedom and their racketeering activities."

"All good, Dr. Joe, you've got us all fully committed to your plans. I know we're in safe hands." Irma nodded and looked at both Stephen and Sharon to ensure that they agreed also. Both confirmed with head nods.

"Great" I continued. "First and foremost there can be absolutely no contact with anyone you currently know. I will keep your own phones safely locked away at my place not far from here. The mobiles you have are for between us only and another emergency number I'll give you for while I'm away in Italy." Everyone nodded.

"Who's the emergency contact?" Stephen
asked

"Michael Jones. He's a local cop. My dad
taught him everything he knows about policing. He's
totally trustworthy, but we don't want to involve too
many people at the moment, so only in emergencies
as I said."

"I think we are all ok with that. The kids may
baulk at not being able to speak to their friends but
we'll manage that." Stephen now the spokesperson
for the others agreed. "What else?"

"You have to promise me that there will be
no trips off these premises. Infanta doesn't know
where you are, but if you put in appearances out
there, well who knows the ways and means he has to
try and locate you. I know it will be very difficult,
but there's enough food both fresh and otherwise in
the fridge and the pantry for even later than when I
return from Italy."

They all nodded again their acceptance.

"When will you be back from Italy?" Sharon
asked

"Dr. Joe will be back in time to take me to
see my Joe on Tuesday." Irma stepped in. "We can
all trust Dr. Joe, he is a good man." She added.

"Do you think you will be able to help get dad's conviction quashed and him out of prison Joe? He didn't do the things they said he did, I know he didn't. Dad hasn't got a mean bone in his body." Stephen said, he was starting to look worried and tired.

"Look Stephen, as I've said to your mother already, I am going to do my best to help get you guys rid of Infanta's hold on your family. What that best ultimately results in, I can't say for sure at the moment. I can see that you're all good people and deserve all the help I can give you. All I can promise though is as I said, that I WILL do my best."

Irma touched my arm and gave me a warm smile. "Dr. Joe, I just hope things work out for you and Miss Samantha. She is very different from her uncle that girl of yours, you both deserve better than Mr. Infanta." She paused, "I'm off to bed now, that's if there is nothing more to discuss."

Returning the smile I told her, "no I think that's all. I'll be back in the morning to see how things are going before I drive to the airport. If you need me in the meantime, you all have my prepaid number."

With that I bade them all a good night and left for my parents place.

Chapter 10.

The next day's events started without any drama.

Visiting the Badgleys straight after breakfast, I took yet another alternative route by going north to Ringwood first, before doubling back and taking different minor roads than I had done yesterday to get to the safe house. Again no one followed me.

Back at the safe house, I first had to work to allay their fears that had increased again overnight.

The children in particular were in a sombre mood, they did not fully understanding why they were there and why they couldn't contact their friends or go for trips. Fortunately I had taken some of my old games to give them. These included a variety of board games, some meccano and an electric car racing set. The children immediately cheered at the sight of the things they could now do to keep themselves occupied.

The three adults only needed a little verbal encouragement to build them up, they not getting quite as down as the children were.

Giving Stephen, Michael Jones' contact number, I suggested he added that contact to all the prepaids 'just in case' and reiterated the need to only call Michael in a real emergency.

I had the idea of leaving the gun I'd found in the wine cellar with him. However the thought played on my mind that Stephen might use it to protect his family or even worse, shooting one of his family members by accident and then being imprisoned with his father for trying to taking the law into his own hands. No, bad idea!

Leaving them with one more assurance of everything going to be ok, I left to pack for Italy and then it was on the road to pick up my passport and a few other things from my own place, not far from Gatwick.

The approximately two hour flight had me landing in Naples at about 7.55p.m., where Sam and her youngest brother Federico were waiting for me.

Federico, a baby faced young man of about twenty years, moved to one side at the baggage claim carousel to allow Sam and I some private catch up time.

And as for Sam, well she was absolutely gorgeous, she was indeed a stunner. And intelligent and 'Miss Personality Plus' and well I could go on and on. Not that I am biased in any way you understand!

There wasn't too long a wait for my bag, which I picked up and we turned to see where Federico was waiting when I thought I saw someone watching us from behind a building support column.

"Sam, just wait there a moment, I need to check something." I told her dropping my bag on the floor.

Rushing to the column, there was no-one there. I looked around but apart from regular airport looking people movement there was nothing suspicious.

"What is wrong?" Federico asked as he and Sam came over to where I stood near the column.

"Oh nothing, I'm probably being a little paranoid. Too little sleep lately and with missing Sam and all that. No, let's get out of here."

Federico seemed appeased at my answer, Sam however still had a slight worried look on her face as we then walked towards the car park and Federico's car.

And I probably didn't help Sam any with my looking over my shoulder from time to time. Just checking no-one was following!

Driving first to the hospital, Sam wanted me to see her mother while she was still with us.

At Mrs. Infanta's bedside as we walked into the private hospital room were Sam's other brothers Giorgio, the oldest of the four siblings and Davide who was about my age. They had been there most of the evening visiting and after introductions, both went outside the room with Federico while Sam and I remained in the room to see Mrs. Infanta.

"Mamma, questo e il mio ragazzo Joe." Sam told her mother as she held her hand. ("Mum, this is my boy Joe.") There was no response from Mrs. Infanta. "È Inglese." Sam added. ("He's English").

Moving over to where Sam was standing I placed my hand on top of Sam's and Mrs. Infanta's hands. "Hello Mrs. Infanta." I said. "It's nice to meet you. You have a wonderful daughter." Sam gave me an elbow dig to the ribs. "Well it's true." I laughed, not being overly comfortable about what to say.

Being already fairly late we decided to leave and return the next day. Giorgio took over as chaperone while Davide and Federico remained at the hospital.

Exiting the hospital we headed for the car park and Giorgio's vehicle when suddenly 'PING', I fell to the ground holding my now painful left shoulder.

Giorgio collected Sam in his arms and dropped them both to the ground, covering her as the brave protective older brother he'd always been.

Looking behind us I saw a man in a dark suit running away from the scene then getting into a large car and driving away.

By that time a small crowd had started to gather, including a couple of security guards in uniform and with guns in hand. One of them blew a whistle, pointing to other security personnel coming out of the hospital to chase after the car.

Standing up, I started to brush myself off when Sam screamed. "Joe you're bleeding, you've been shot!"

I winced as I placed my right hand on my upper left arm. "It's not too bad. I think I'll live." I said.

Giorgio spoke in Italian to one of the security guards, while the other one employed himself in crowd control.

As the security guard spoke on his radio, Giorgio came over to Sam and me.

"Are you ok Joe?" he asked. "Why would anyone want to shoot you, you've only just come into the country?"

"It's just a scratch I think, Giorgio. I'll be fine." I looked towards the returning guards who hadn't been able to catch up with the escaping gunman. "I don't know who that was or why they would want to take a shot at me. That's if I was the target and it's not just a case of mistaken identity." I didn't want to tell anyone yet about what was happening in England. That revelation would be happening soon.

"Darling, let's have you back inside to get someone to look at your wound." Sam said nervously. There were a few tears starting to well in the corner of her eyes.

"Don't worry love. I'll be fine."

"The security guard has radioed for the police. They'll be here very soon. Let's get inside everyone, it'll be safer there." Giorgio suggested. "The police will need as much information as we can give them and the security staff are taking down the details of the potential witnesses."

"Welcome to Italy Joe Bedford." I muttered, ok a little sarcastically!

I put on a brave face as we walked back inside the hospital, my arm hurting more than I'd have liked to admit to those around me.

Inside we were led to a treatment room and I stripped off my jacket and shirt, letting a male nurse clean and examine the wound. He then left to report his triage assessment to a doctor.

Through the window I saw a couple of 'Polizia' vehicles race up to the front door and two officers getting out from each.

The nurse came back with a doctor just as the police also entered into the room.

While Giorgio spoke to the police, Sam translated for me to the medical staff.

"It's all good Joe. Just a graze they said. The nurse is going to clean and dress the wound for you and then as far as they're concerned you can go." She turned and thanked the doctor who left alongside the nurse who presumably went to get the dressing.

Giorgio turned to us as the polizia left the room. "They're going to speak to any witnesses Joe and then get copies of the security footage from the cameras outside." He told us. "We have to go straight to the police station when we're finished here to give statements."

We both nodded our understanding. "Before we actually get to the police station, I need to talk to you both." I offered not being one hundred percent sure of Giorgio, but I knew how close he and Sam were so - time to bite the bullet, if you'll forgive the pun!

The nurse returned and cleaned and dressed the wound, offering me some pain killers which I refused. I then re-dressed and we cautiously walked to Giorgio's car to sit there for a chat.

"What's going on Joe?" Sam asked looking very concerned.

Looking from Sam to Giorgio and then back to Sam again, I began the story.

"As you know Sam, I've been working on some pretty secretive equipment. Sorry Giorgio, but I can't give you the full details yet, hopefully one day. Sam you know the whole story up to where you came to see your mum about ten days ago."

Taking a deep breath I continued, "Your uncle, Lorenzo, somehow got to know about my work and asked me to use the equipment for, let me say – to feather his own nest."

"What!" Sam exclaimed. "I knew he could be sly and greedy at times, but I didn't think he would stoop so low."

"Yes, I don't know how much you really know him Joe, but uncle Lorenzo has some bad criminal associates."

"Giorgio how could you say such a thing! He's paid for all my education and has kept me for the last ten years, since the accident." Sam defended her uncle referring to the accident that killed their father and put Mrs. Infanta in the coma.

"Sam." He reached out to the back seat and picked up her free hand. I was holding the other! "It's true," he continued. "Uncle Lorenzo I've learnt over the past few years has many fingers pointing at him, especially from the polizia. I didn't want to tell you because, well you met Joe here and I thought you would be separating yourself from Lorenzo eventually."

Sam stopped shaking her head after the initial denial. "Well ok, it's a bit hard to swallow, but! So Joe, what's happening, please continue?"

"Well after a couple of 'trips' to help with Lorenzo's needs." I gestured with two fingers of both hands some 'air quotation marks', "things started to get a little hot. Now two of his staff members are missing and I know of at least one other, Marco has been shot dead." I didn't mention other names or indeed the fact that one of those missing was still back in 1698.

Both Sam and Giorgio looked rather pensive as they reflected on what I was telling them.

"Another staff member has asked me for help to get away from your uncle," I continued, "and there are some serious goings on in that situation as well."

"So what are we going to do now?" Sam asked. Realization beginning to set in that uncle Lorenzo wasn't so sweet after all!

"Well first we have to get to the police station to give them statements about what happened here at the hospital. I don't know how much to give them about uncle Lorenzo, but I'll get my brain into gear as we drive there and hopefully come up with something."

"Oh Joe, what a mess," Sam gave me a big hug. Now that I had told them about their uncle, I was relieved to see that Sam still loved me. It almost didn't matter about all those other things anymore!

Giorgio turned to face the car's windscreen and he started the car.

"OK Joe, better get that thinking cap on, here we go to the polizia."

Chapter 11.

We had been directed to go to the Polizia di stato in Vicaria, a district of Naples.

It wasn't too far but Giorgio drove slowly to allow me to get my thoughts together. He parked the car about 30 metres from the police building and we sat for a while inside the car.

"I think your two statements should just concern the incident at the hospital. I'm going to add a few suspicions about what's happening in England without going into too much detail. I believe your uncle's man Tommaso, he could have been our shooter. I don't know his surname only that he lives here in Italy somewhere. I'll mention his name and what little I know of his relationship with Lorenzo in my statement. That also means we might need some help from the police if he is involved."

Both Sam and Giorgio accepted this. However Giorgio added, "You must be careful Joe, at least until we know who we can fully trust. Italian police can sometimes be on the bad guy's payroll."

"There are some of that kind of police world over Giorgio, but yes I will be careful."

We got out of the car and walked into the police station, where Giorgio reported who we were at the front desk.

The officer Giorgio spoke to, opened the access door to the interview rooms and pointed to one room in particular. "Per favore aspetta te qui. Qualcuno verrà a parlare con voi presto." ("Please wait in here. Someone will come to speak with you soon.").

As we sat down on three standard waiting room style chairs, the officer closed the door as he left us alone in the room.

Sparsely furnished, the room contained several more similar style chairs, a medium sized desk with a phone and recording equipment on it. High in one corner was a security camera with its red light flashing and a large, presumably two way mirror filling one wall. It made me feel like I was the bad guy.

Waiting about twenty minutes we exchanged small talk with lots of cuddles and kisses in between. That's only between Sam and I you understand, not me and Giorgio! Just more catching up on lost time.

Then, suddenly the door opened and a well-dressed though un-shaven man holding a file marched in followed by two other men wearing dark blue jackets with 'NCB' logo patches sewn to the upper arms. Both these were armed.

The man in the suit put the file on the desk and held out his hand to each of us in turn. "Sorry to keep you all waiting. My name is Malcolm Brunelli. I'm an officer of the S. C. I. P., the International Police Cooperation Service. These two junior officers work for the National Central Bureau. Basically we're representing Interpol."

We all said hello to Brunelli, who spoke English without any trace of an accent and we nodded to the junior officers.

Brunelli opened the file half way and then closed it again to look at his watch. "Look I realize that you all and you in particular Dr. Bedford, have had a bit of a stressful day." He acknowledged, looking straight at me. We hadn't given him our individual names and I got the strange feeling that he'd been investigating or had known about us for some time!

"How about we do this in the morning? These two boys will escort you all to your home in Chiaia, Signor Infanta. I trust Dr. Bedford IS staying at your place?" Brunelli said.

"It seems you know much about us already Mr. Brunelli." I replied.

"Only a little," He lied "but we can get better acquainted in the morning. Your wound is only superficial the hospital tells me Dr. Bedford and we will provide security for you as I've already hinted." He stretched and yawned. "Again I apologize but as you see coming in from the U.K. yesterday morning and not having slept or refreshed myself since then, it maybe be better for all of us." He lifted his jacket and sniffed in the direction of his armpit, which made Sam crack a huge smile and she turned away in an attempt to hide her amusement.

"I still feel you know a lot more than you're telling us - like how did you know that I was Dr. Bedford, with all respect that is." I replied standing my ground.

Now it was his turn to smile. "What a perceptive man you are Dr. Bedford. Yes we've, that's my team both here and in England, have been following Lorenzo Infanta and his little schemes for a few years now. So as you see, there is no need for regulatory statements concerning the shooting. As for knowing which of you gentlemen was Dr. Bedford and which was Giorgio Infanta," He pointed to my injured arm, "a certain hole in your jacket was a bit of a giveaway! In fact I can reveal to you that the man who fired the gun in your direction was a certain Matteo Lombardi, a local resident here in Napoli. He works for your uncle or indeed anyone who offers him the right deal." He turned to look at Sam and Giorgio as he said the last few words.

Sam put her hand to her mouth in an expression of shock, the merriment fully vanquished.

"Shall we say nine o'clock tomorrow then? The two officers, who'll replace these ones, will bring you to a temporary office we have set up in a home in Vomero. So please, until then." He gestured towards the door.

Looking at each other we all nodded and walked out of the room, followed closely by the two NCB officers, leaving Brunelli in the interview room alone.

Approaching Giorgio's block of flats, the garage security door slowly raised and we waited in silence for it to give us enough room to drive in.

The NCB officers who had parked in front of the flats, got out of their vehicle while we waited for the garage door. One stayed outside at the front entrance while the second disappeared inside.

After parking in the basement car park, we climbed several flights of white stone stairs to reach Giorgio's home, the penthouse suite.

The second NCB officer was already standing guard at Giorgio's front door.

"Thorough!" I exclaimed looking at him as I followed Giorgio and Sam inside after the door was unlocked.

There was no response from the man.

Giorgio showed me where my room was. Okay, you're probably thinking that I should have been sleeping with Sam in her room. After all we'd had a strong love interest going now for about four months. Well I'm pleased to inform you all that we'd both agreed not to, well you know what – until we were married!

Frustrating? Yes very. Old fashioned? Maybe, but we'd both had relationships before we'd met each other that had been of a physical nature. Each had been hurt in those relationships and it's not as if we hadn't enjoyed that aspect of those relationships, but for THIS relationship both of us were convinced that first had to come our friendship and compatibility, then commitment and marriage and then - boy that's going to be a good night! I was going to propose here in Italy before all this palaver with Lorenzo Infanta had started, I even had the engagement ring with me; so as soon as things are all sorted…..

Alright, now we've gotten that out of the way, let's get back to the story.

Outside, the building Giorgio lived in looked quaint and old. By huge contrast the inside of the penthouse was affluent, bright and very modern. Every room had stunning views, of the city on one side and the bay and sweeping coastline on the other, the city's night lights being particularly enchanting.

The furnishings were very up-market. A large open planned area with fine white leather plush seating to one side, with a magnificent ornate glass and marble dining table and a professionally fitted kitchen with walk-in pantry and separate scullery on the other side. Off the long wide hallway were four bedrooms, all with ensuite facilities, a grand office/study, a gym/sauna room and a large games room which then opened out onto a huge outdoor entertaining area. Very Impressive! Giorgio was doing very well for himself in the online retail business.

Sitting outside on one of the balconies with some light refreshments, we needed to have some serious chat.

"How could I have been so blind?" Sam said, examining her own naivety. "He even tried to have my own boyfriend killed right in front of me.

For ten years I was there living under the same roof - that **Don** Lorenzo lived in!" Her voice told me that she was getting angry at herself.

"But Sam love, he purposely hid it from you. You can't blame yourself." I defended her. "And look, at me, I'm the one who fell afoul of his scheming lies and helped him with some ill-gotten gains. And I'm supposed to be the brainy one of the family!"

She hit me playfully but hard.

"Hey that's not nice, hitting an already injured man." I joked. "Good job it wasn't the other arm you hit."

"Well I can remedy that Joe Bedford if you want me to." She leaned over so as to hit me again, but this time planted a kiss on my cheek instead.

"OK, I submit, you win. I can't take any more. You're the brainy one I admit it." She laughed and tweaked my nose.

"Come on you two, I thought I was the chaperone, not the babysitter." Giorgio laughed with us.

I looked at Sam, she was gorgeous. Long black hair, pretty facial features including delightfully sexy hazel coloured eyes which she could cross when pulling a funny face. You guys reading this can probably tell - I was smitten!

"Hey Joe, how did you help Lorenzo with some 'ill-gotten gains?'" Giorgio interrupted my thoughts.

Sam and I looked at each other and we nodded in unison, time to tell Giorgio the whole story.

"Well to cut a long story short, I invented a time travel method and was going to use it to help people when Lorenzo somehow found out about it. He enlisted me go back with one of his henchmen to Pompeii, just before Vesuvius erupted, to bring forward in time some precious articles to sell at huge prices. That trip didn't help Lorenzo's bank balance any, so next we went back to 1698 and Whitehall Palace just before a fire destroyed it." While Sam looked enthralled at the details I hadn't previously furnished her about, she was hardly able to contain herself. Giorgio however looked blank faced and just listened intently as he leaned forward in his seat.

I continued. "Things went wrong on the second trip also and I had to leave Carlos, my 'body guard', behind back in 1698 to face two sword wielding palace guards. When I returned to the current time period, Luigi, Lorenzo's new 2IC and even Lorenzo himself didn't seem to care what had happened to Carlos, as some other major issue had arisen. Marco was shot dead in the study and after his body was loaded into one of the cars, they all left which enabled me to escape."

Sitting back in his chair, Giorgio closed his eyes for about thirty seconds, remaining silent. After reopening his eyes he shook his head and said to me, "Ok Joe, don't tell me." He put his glass down and stood up, walking over to the balcony rail to look over towards the city whose lights were rapidly starting to be turned off, one by one.

"What's your story for Brunelli tomorrow? He asked me.

"Giorgio, Joe DID invent time travel. I've seen some of his experiments, it's amazing!" Sam's turn to defend me now. "How exciting Joe." She cried with glee, focusing attention back in my direction. "What was it like, Pompeii I mean? Oh wow Joe it sounds fantastic, you actually went back in time."

"The real trick was getting back in one piece. And I think that's going to have to be my new regular party trick from now on, surviving in one piece!"

Giorgio returned to his seat. "You mean you actually did these things Joe?" He queried, starting to get some look of belief on his face.

I nodded. "Yes Giorgio, I'm telling you the truth."

Shaking his head this time in amazement, "So I ask again. What are you going to tell Brunelli tomorrow?"

He sat back in his chair and let out a big sigh.

Sam and I copied his example, sitting back and sighing together. "Yes, what indeed do I tell him?"

Chapter 12

At Brunelli's temporary office in Vomero, a nice looking villa style home, we were led to a comfortable boardroom setting in what used to be a lounge area, by an NCB officer. Brunelli already sat waiting there along with a smartly dressed older woman, perhaps about sixty, sixty five but very elegant looking.

He stood up as we entered and held his hand out to each one of us in turn. Then turning to the woman he introduced her to us as Assistant Director of Investigations Coralie Walsh representing the U.K.'s National Crime Agency.

After the greeting he invited us to sit, offering refreshments as needed by pointing to a coffee and tea making station at one end of the room.

"Now," he began. "Let's get down to business. Ms. Walsh has given me a complete update as to all her department knows about Lorenzo Infanta and his operation both here and in the UK. Including concerning a man you must both know Dr. Bedford, Miss Infanta. That man was known to you as Marco Guarente and to us as undercover agent Daniel Phillips. We also have reason to believe that Agent Phillips is now dead having had no reports from him in the last three days."

"Lorenzo Infanta has been on our radar for quite some time now." Ms. Walsh added. "Illegal drugs and weapons dealing, grand larceny, murder are just some of his groups usual pursuits. And more recently we've added people trafficking and slavery. Your uncle is building quite a reputation with us!" She summated, saying the last comment directly to both Sam and Giorgio who sat eyes wide open.

"And here on the continent, virtually the same picture." Brunelli came in, both acting as a well-oiled information team. "Europol have reported his dealings in seven other countries with activities of similar nature to those already mentioned. They are letting my office take the lead in the investigations, but as you can appreciate, many people are wanting to put an end to Lorenzo Infanta's business as soon as possible."

"We are hoping", Brunelli continued. "That you Dr. Bedford could help us with a little more evidence and testimony to edge us a little closer towards the mass arrest of the whole group."

After a brief pause, Brunelli turned to face Giorgio. "Senor Infanta, my office has fully investigated your side of the family and we can honestly say that all we've found are A1 model citizens. You and your brothers are a credit to your country. I'm glad to say it seems that uncle Lorenzo is the only black sheep in the family." Giorgio nodded his appreciation as Brunelli continued.

"We had a tail on Matteo Lombardi, the shooter at the hospital and have video evidence of his attempt to kill you Dr. Bedford."

"Do you mean you just stood by watching while he shot me!" I stood up enraged. "I could have been killed man. What on earth…"

"Now, now Dr. Bedford. We did distract Lombardi enough for his shot to miss your heart completely." Brunelli interrupted waving both his hands palm down in a 'calm down movement'. "Senor Lombardi is, unfortunately for all his victims at least, one of the most accurate gunmen in Europe. If we HADN'T intervened precisely the time and way we did, you definitely would be dead by now."

Sitting down I offered an "ok, thanks, I think. Yes thank you and your team, it seems I was a little hasty with my analysis."

"Our pleasure Dr. Bedford, all is forgiven. We do try to please as best we can." Brunelli smirked.

"Do you know anything about a man named Tommaso?" I asked.

"That'll be Tommaso Moretti." Walsh answered. "Another very dangerous man. Perhaps even more so than Lombardi, who's basically just a hired gun. Moretti on the other hand is a ruthless leader as Lorenzo Infanta's protégé"

"Moretti worked for Lorenzo in England before returning here some years ago to head Lorenzo's overseas operations. Ms. Walsh and her department were investigating a particular double murder he was suspected of committing back in the U.K. in which subsequent new evidence arose which pointed the finger elsewhere."

"As you know Malcolm, that new evidence appearing when it did, just didn't seem right. I know a man was convicted on it, but I wasn't happy at all that the case proceeded as it did. I still think Moretti was the real killer, it's just a gut feeling I had then and still have now." Walsh said patting her clenched fist on her stomach.

"That convicted man wouldn't be an Englishman named Joe Badgley would it?" I asked

Walsh and Brunelli nodded, "How do know that Dr. Bedford?" Brunelli asked.

"I'm booked to visit him at Strangeways Prison on Tuesday. His wife Irma wants me to help them out with trying to get the verdict reversed."

"Interesting." Brunelli reflected looking first at Walsh then back to me. "Irma Badgley asked you for help against Lorenzo Infanta? The Badgley's are deeply entrenched in this crime syndicate, almost as much as Lorenzo himself. She's also been missing in the last few days. We suspect she's gone into hiding."

"Never! Are we talking about the same little old lady, Mr. Infanta's cook?" I was incredulous.

"Joe, may I call you Joe?" Brunelli asked learning forward in my direction.

"Yes of course, it is my name after all. I just can't believe I could have assessed her so mistakenly."

"Joe, we all make mistakes. I myself almost fell for her innocent old lady charm when in London three weeks ago. One of my men was with me on a stakeout at her son Stephen's home. We had the place bugged and were listening in to their plans to break Joe Badgley out of prison, Luigi was with them. It was him that had driven her to Manchester that day from the Infanta house. Stephen drove off in his car somewhere, so my partner followed him while I stayed behind to keep observing Irma and Luigi.

I thought I heard gun fire and went to investigate when they both exited the house and I had to hurriedly run to hide at the side of the property. Luigi got into the car but Irma must have heard me so she pulled out a gun and started to look where I was hiding. If it wasn't for Luigi shouting that the noise she'd heard must have been a fox or something, I might not have been here to tell the story. No believe me Joe, Irma Badgley is one of the worst kinds!"

Brunelli finished his story and I turned to look at Sam who looked just as bewildered at this new information concerning Mrs. Badgley as I was.

"Malcolm, how is it I've not heard this tale before? Where is the report?" Walsh asked Brunelli.

"I filed it only this Tuesday. It's in the pipeline Coralie, I'm sure you'll get to see it soon. So Joe, do you have any idea where Irma Badgley is now?" Brunelli inquired.

"She's in a safe house together with Stephen and his family. I was the one who arranged everything for them all to stay there, away from Lorenzo's clutches until we could sort a few things out."

"You'd better tell me where the house is Joe. I can get a couple of cars around there to have them arrested tonight."

"NO!" Walsh interrupted. "Walls have ears Malcolm. We don't want anyone to inform them before we can get there and then have them disappear yet again. We'll leave them there for the time being, and I think I might have a plan to lead them right into enough evidence to secure their convictions."

Now I was totally spaced out. Irma Badgley was 'one of the worst kinds'! Stephen Badgley was also in on the act. I even thought Brunelli had seniority over Walsh, now even that had changed in the last few seconds.

Standing, I walked over to the coffee table and poured myself a large strong mug full of brewed coffee. Pity there wasn't anything stronger! "Anyone else for a drink?" I offered.

"Not for me." Sam replied, "Besides I may just choke on it. I think I need to digest all this first."

Brunelli and Giorgio also declined my offer, but Walsh got up and walked towards me at the coffee table.

As she made herself a drink, she deliberately nudged me so that I spilt coffee on my trousers.

"Oh Joe, so clumsy of me, I do apologize. Malcolm, do be a darling and show Joe where he can get cleaned up please."

Brunelli escorted me to the bathroom, leaving Walsh with Sam and Giorgio for about five minutes.

"Can't take you anywhere." Sam said as Brunelli and I returned to the interview room.

She was obviously feeling a little more relaxed than when we'd left the room.

The conversation continued for another hour.

We talked about Luigi some more, Danny and Carlos and others in the Infanta crime family.

Interestingly, I learned that Carlos had been asked to kill Marco, but had refused, giving excuses each time Lorenzo had commissioned him to do the job. I don't fully understand how they knew these facts apart from maybe Marco perhaps had bugged the mansion in Virginia Water.

But I did understand now as to why Infanta and Luigi weren't that concerned when Carlos had been left behind in 1698 to face his likely death. They would have killed him for not doing his job even if he'd have returned with me anyway.

I still hadn't told them about time travelling and didn't intend to either. Some things just have to be kept quiet. 'Science is for scientists' I always told my students.

Walsh had suggested that Sam and I returned to England that very afternoon, but Sam refused to leave her mother.

It was agreed then that Walsh, Brunelli and myself would return that evening.

It had taken quite a bit of persuading to get me to leave Sam again, but Walsh convinced me that I was vital in her plans for further arrests in England and it would be the safest option all round having all of them locked up ASAP and end the matter once and for all. She also offered tripling the security detail for Sam and her brothers until everything was settled.

Brunelli also didn't want to go, but this one Walsh won solely on rank.

Walsh said her goodbyes to Sam and Giorgio, saying she would see me at the airport later. Then she went off to arrange the extra manpower. Brunelli, looking quite deflated said he was going off to get some lunch.

We left the office with our upsized entourage and headed for the hospital to see Mrs. Infanta.

After about another hour there, talking little of that morning's events, Sam and I also went to find something to eat and to get some time alone, leaving Giorgio at the hospital with his mother.

We managed to get a quiet corner table inside 'Il Comandante'. Though neither of us were particularly hungry, the food was divine and the quiet setting really lent itself to what I next had in mind.

"Sam, before all this chaos with uncle Lorenzo, I had in mind to take our relationship to the next step." Sam's eyes lit up. "We don't know what's going to happen over the next few days and the timing maybe utterly wrong but.." I knelt on one knee in front of her holding both her hands in mine. "We might not get another chance so, Samantha Infanta – will you be my wife?" I reached into my jacket pocket and pulled out the ring box.

Sam took it from me and opened it, her whole face now brighter than last night's city lights.

She took out the rose gold diamond studded Victorian engagement ring and tried it on her ring finger. It fitted perfectly!

"Oh Joe, it won't come off, it's stuck. I guess I'll HAVE to say yes now!" She broke into the biggest smile and wrapped her arms around me. "Of course it's yes, what took you so long Dr. Bedford?"

We kissed passionately oblivious to all around us - that was until the whole restaurant broke out into cheering and applause, even the NCB officers on guard at the door were smiling.

Standing up, I left more than double the food bill on the table, then taking my fiancé's hand we started to walk out of the restaurant. The restaurant manager approached us at the door with a bottle of champagne. "Mi permettetemi essere il primo a congratularvi." ("Allow me to be the first to congratulate you both.") He said and then proceeded to give first Sam then me a big hug and a kiss on both cheeks for each of us.

Brunelli's men stepped closer, unsure whether this might be an attack. "Easy boys!" I placated them. "He's only being nice, no problema qui."

The manager continued his excited congratulations by enthusiastically shaking our hands with a huge smile on his face. Then after a real bitter look at the NCB men, returned to his restaurant duties.

Outside we walked slowly in each other arms for a while, two NCB men at a discreet distance behind us and two more in a car driving alongside almost parallel.

We talked about the good future we hoped we had. We didn't mention the alternative future if something went wrong with the uncle Lorenzo saga, at all!

Returning to Giorgio's place, he told us that Coralie Walsh had texted him to tell me that she'd booked a flight back to London for us and to meet at the airport at 4p.m.

Sam showed Giorgio the ring and after hugging her strongly but lovingly for about thirty seconds, he reached out an arm to include myself in a group hug.

"You'd better go pack Joe if you're going to catch that flight." He advised.

At the airport we said our goodbyes. That was extremely hard, especially not knowing what the near future had in-store for us.

"Joe come back to me." Sam said. "I don't want to be a widow before even getting married." Tears welled in her beautiful eyes.

"Don't worry my love. Our wedding day is one date I'm definitely not going to miss. Try and keep those brothers of yours in line while I'm gone. I love you, just remember that and forget everything else until we're together again, ok?"

She tried to smile but did a terrible job. I kissed her and was still hugging her as Walsh strode up to where we were standing.

"No more time for that Dr. Bedford. We've got a plane to catch, let's go."

I doubted she'd ever been so in love herself.

A final kiss for Sam and a hand shake for Giorgio, "Take good care of her my brother." I told him.

Then I waved goodbye and followed Walsh out to the tarmac where a private jet was waiting. This lady had some clout!

Climbing up the steps to get on the plane, I turned to see Sam and Giorgio waving at one of the terminal windows. I returned the wave and entered the plane. I suddenly felt that I didn't want to go, no matter whose lives my return to London might save. All I wanted to do was stay with Sam.

On the plane, Brunelli was already seated, strapped in and looking down in the mouth. I chose

a quiet seat away from the others and fastened my
belt as the plane started to taxi towards the runway.

Chapter 13.

Back in 1698, Carlos and I tried not to show too much fear as we stood swords in hand ready to defend ourselves. "We are the king's men." I shouted. It was no good, the lead guard rallied forward with some intent. Carlos blocked the first blow but was unable to withstand the slice of the second guard whose sword cut Carlos open like he was a piece of Swiss cheese. I just stood there thinking I was a scientist not a swashbuckler. The guards turned my way with the same murderous look of intent that they'd given Carlos.

All of a sudden an earthquake shook and the very ground gave way beneath my feet.

Opening my eyes, I realized – it was just a dream. "Sorry for the rough landing folks," came the pilot's announcement.

Rubbing the sleep from my face, I stretched and yawned. Looking through the window of the plane, we'd arrived not at Gatwick or another main airport, but at a much smaller airstrip that was unknown to me.

As the plane came to a stop, the others started to rise from their seats so I followed their example, with just a little more concern regarding Carlos' safety on my mind.

Outside was very warm still, unusually so. "Looks like we're in for an Indian summer again Dr. Bedford. But then I think I heard somewhere that you rather like the warmer conditions." Walsh commented as we walked towards a couple of awaiting cars and their drivers.

"Yes, give me 110 degrees any day." I answered casually. "Where exactly are we Ms. Walsh?"

"This is an old RAF base Dr. Bedford. We acquired it a few years ago in order to facilitate speedier movement in and out of Europe. No passport or luggage checks to worry about. Senor Brunelli is going in one car to his hotel, but we need to have a few things arranged before we meet up tomorrow for a full briefing. The real action will start after that my good Dr."

Our driver took us to a warehouse just a few miles from the airstrip. Various road signs suggested we were perhaps somewhere in Hertfordshire.

The warehouse we were driven to was a well-guarded place without any signage as to what went on inside.

We parked after being checked in at the gate and were then escorted by a security officer to the main door. Opening the door and saluting, presumably to Assistant Director Walsh, he then left as we went inside.

Walsh signed in at the unattended front desk and then she guided me over to a lift, and used a security I.D. tag to call the lift car. While we waited I took a look around the place. It was very bare, no pictures, logos, chairs, in fact none of the comforts or necessities you'd find in a similar commercial type property with the exception of the front desk and sign in pad. There wasn't even a receptionist in sight. There was, I noticed however, complete coverage of the foyer by security cameras!

"After you Dr. Bedford." She waved me into the lift when it had arrived, then when we were both inside she used both a retina scan and keyed in a pin number to activate the floor level control.

Down we went. It was difficult to tell how many floors we descended, but I roughly calculated about enough time for the average lift to drop about twenty levels during that same time period. We were deep underground!

The lift door opened up to a laboratory not much different from my own back at Cavendish.

Several people in lab coats ignored us entirely as we walked through to an office at the back of the lab where the door was already open.

A quite burley man in his fifties, also dressed in a lab coat was sitting in a wheelchair filing some papers into a three drawer metal filing cabinet as we went in.

"Ah Ms. Walsh, good to see you again and this must be the famous Dr. Livingston I presume, I mean Bedford of course." He laughed at his own joke and then smiled warmly and offered his hand which I shook. "Sorry don't mind me, but I've always wanted to say that!"

"Please call me Joe." I suggested then asked "and you are Henry Morton Stanley – I presume?"

"Oh he's good Coralie, very good!"

" Sorry Joe, manners evade us somewhat after so many years working down here. This is Dr. Dylan Burrows." Walsh answered for him.

"Or just plain old Dylan - at your service Joe. I've been an admirer of your work at Cavendish for some time. I even have one of your post-graduate students working for me in the lab one floor up." He pointed towards the ceiling.

"Oh, which student, I've had quite a few very bright people go through my hands in the few years I've been lecturing at Cavendish?"

"Sorry Joe, not allowed to tell anyone. We'd have to lock you up for twenty years in isolation if you found out." Dylan laughed again, even louder this time.

"Some of us have gotten used to Dylan and his humour over the years Dr. Bedford, but unfortunately I'm not one of them." Walsh said solemnly.

Dylan 'Mr. Stanley' Burrows gave a dry smile to end that particular interchange.

"Please take a seat." He bent forward to remove some files that lay on one of the visitor chairs, placing them on the desk. We sat as my mind raced around his words, 'an admirer of my work'. Did he know about my time travel experiments?

"You're an admirer of my work, as a lecturer you mean?" I enquired carefully.

"Yes that, but mainly your thesis on quantum reflectivity. Superb work Joe, absolutely superb. I even asked the powers that be to try and recruit you for working here after I'd read that. They said that you were a definite target for the future."

"As long as I'm not a target for any gunman to take a potshot at!"

"I know what you mean." He laughed again. "Pity you didn't take your thesis any further though!"

If only he knew!

"Please gentlemen." Walsh interrupted. " We have only a little time in which to do business, perhaps we can leave this conversation for another day. Dylan, were you able to complete that certain task for me?"

"Yes, Coralie, and I'm very happy to announce it all works splendidly." He reached into in a draw and pulled out a large brown paper envelope. "We've fully tested it in the lab and it now awaits its first field mission."

"I'm sorry, I seem to have missed a few beats here. What are we talking about.?"

"Dr. Bedford, please open the envelope. This is a special gift we have for you, although I must admit that we didn't have you in mind specifically when Dr. Burrows initiated its development."

At Walsh's beckoning, I opened the package and pulled out a necktie.

"Thanks, I love the blue, though I'm not too sure about the paisley design."

"Joe." Dylan exclaimed with an exuberant enthusiasm which I felt was a bit of overkill at the time. "That is not just a necktie." He took the tie off me. "This is the very latest in nanotechnology photographic equipment! This is a major breakthrough in spyware. This is the future, right here and now!"

"Dr. Bedford, a camera and microphone are interwoven into the fabric of the tie." Walsh stated. "It will record both sound and vision and relay them to our observation desks, from anywhere in the world. And look," she grabbed one end of the tie while Dylan still held on tight to the other. They pulled as if in a varsity tug of war match.

Stopping after a good two minutes, they passed the tie back to me. It should have at least been stretched out of shape, even maybe have been ripped in two, but no, it looked brand new.

"And!" Walsh said taking the tie back off me. She picked up a lighter from off the desk and triggered a large flame, applying it to the tie.

After about 30 seconds, she returned the tie to me again for examination. It was unscathed, no sign of any burns or even any congealing of the fibers. In fact no marks or damage whatsoever.

"Very impressive" I admitted. "But what does… Oh hold on a moment, I see what you're up to. You want me to do some dirty work for you using this to record whatever that may be."

"Dr. Bedford please, it's not dirty work as you call it. Its vital surveillance work, something that your king and country will be extremely grateful for. Something that none of us could do as competently, only you are in this unique position to be able to get the evidence we need."

"I've just gotten engaged. This," I held up the tie," and what you want me to do will more likely get me killed. No I'm sorry Ms. Walsh, you have the wrong man!"

"Dr. Bedford, believe me – You are the ONLY one who can do it. And please be assured we will have your back, all the way. Without you, Infanta and the vast majority of his gang will get clean away with not only what you already know they've done, but with many other horrendous crimes. You don't want that, do you Joe?" That was the first and only time she addressed me by my first name.

"Damn you Walsh. Something tells me that you already know I'm going to do it. But mark my words, as soon as this is over, I'm out of here, its addio, au revoir, sayonara – you understand?"

"Perfectly Dr. Bedford, if that's what you want. I'm sure all will be well and you and Miss Samantha will be able to enjoy many happy years together making bambini e bambine! Oh and Dr. Bedford, mums the word. Not a single person outside this room now can know about the tie or what you and I will discuss when we move back upstairs. Not Malcolm Brunelli, not Samantha – absolutely no-one."

After reluctantly agreeing, we said our goodbyes to Dylan and went back up in the lift, the tie in my jacket pocket.

As we travelled to a higher level I posed a rather satirical question to Walsh. "So perhaps I should call you 'M" and Dylan 'Q' from now on?"

"Perhaps!" Walsh actually cracked a smile. "But 007 doesn't suit you at all Dr. Bedford. You're too much of a one girl man, a gentleman should I say. Bond is so fickle in his escapades with the ladies!"

I returned her smile. Maybe she wasn't that hardhearted a person after all.

❖

Actually, Coralie Walsh's 'normality' continued as we settled into yet another office environment, a swankier largish affair with a nice desk, leather seating and some tasteful contemporary artwork on the walls.

"Are you hungry Dr. Bedford?" She asked. "I can order pizza if you like, marinara sound good to you?"

"My favourite, but then it doesn't surprise me that you would know that about me Ms. Walsh."

"I'm not in the game of surprises Dr. Bedford, I'm in the game of knowing and acting on what I know. Was that a yes to the pizza?"

"Indeed it is Ms. Walsh, thank you, and since we're about to share pizza together maybe we can be a little less informal, Joe will be fine."

"You may call me Coralie, Ms. Walsh or even Assistant Director as per your choice Dr. Bedford, but as for my addressing you, well you will always be Dr. Bedford. Please take that as my showing you the deepest of respect and nothing else."

"Well I thank you for that, then in return also out of respect on how I perceive your talents and your position as Assistant Director, will of course continue with Ms. Walsh."

Walsh smiled. "Dr. Bedford in the foreseeable future we will, I'm positive, be forming a strong working relationship that I know in years to come, you will reflect back on with pride and fondness."

Her words were a little strange. It was if she knew something that I didn't about what the future held and had forgotten that I was quitting as soon as this affair with Infanta and his group was over. I decided not to dwell on the thought, but this astute lady, yes definitely in her mid-sixties, was certainly starting to grow on me.

"Talking of fondness and while we wait for the pizza, can I just call Samantha to let her know everything is alright?"

"Certainly, but you must use this phone here. For one, your cellphone won't have any reception in here, even though we are currently only three stories underground and two, security protocols demand we use a scrambled secure line from these premises. In the meantime, I'll leave you to have your conversation in private and go and organize the pizza. Please give Miss. Infanta my regards and don't forget, mums the word!" With that she departed from the room and left me to call Sam.

Sam didn't answer her phone, which got me more than a little concerned. I tried Giorgio's number and felt after the length of wait for an answer that the same result was going to ensue, however finally the call was answered.

"Ciao, questo è il numero di telefono di Giorgio. Posso aiutarti, questo è suo fratello Davide." ("Hello, this is Giorgio's phone. Can I help, this is his brother Davide.")

"Davide, its Joe, Joe Bedford. Is Sam or Giorgio there?"

"Ah Joe, il mio inglese erh not good. Un attimo prego chiamo Giorgio."

There was a wait of about two or three minutes while Davide went to get Giorgio.

"Joe, it's Giorgio, so sorry my brother, I was with Sam. She's now gone into the ladies powder room to refresh herself after a few tears."

"Giorgio, what's happening over there is it your mother? Has she passed?"

"No Joe, she is still with us in one respect. The doctors have just informed us that it's time to turn off the life machine that keeps mamma breathing. Of course while we knew this moment was going to come, it is still very much a shock. Sam will be fine, they want for one of us to turn the switch, some sort of acceptance of the fact they can't do anymore for her, but I've told them she'll go when she is ready to go."

"Giorgio, I know how vigilant and caring that you've all been with her over the years since the accident. But yes she is still your mother, so I'm the one who should be sorry - that I can't be with you at this time, but please be assured of my love and concern for you all. I know you will take care of Sam for me, but please tell her that I love her and will call her tomorrow, I know it's starting to get late over there."

"It's only 8.45, and Sam is very tired but I think this might be one of the nights where sleep will evade us. You can try again later this evening."

"I don't know if I can Giorgio, but if I can, I will. Just in case though, please give her my message."

"Understood Joe, not a problem. You take care, we will hear from you either later or tomorrow, Ciao brother." He hung up as Ms. Walsh came back into the room pushing a stainless steel butlers trolley filled with four cloches and whatever was underneath them.

"Our kitchen staff, Dr. Bedford, produces I'm sure you'll agree, some exquisite meals." Walsh lifted one of the cloches, revealing a large piece of delicious looking seafood pizza accompanied by a fresh summer salad and a few potato wedges."

"Wow, I thought we were getting pizza delivered in a box by Papa John's or Pizza Hut, this looks like a five star restaurant quality meal! I lifted another cloche to reveal extra pieces of pizza.

"And under here ," Walsh said lifting another cloche, "voila, raspberry and chocolate mousse, one of my personal favourites. Please be seated Dr. Bedford, and enjoy." She motioned that I should sit on the leather lounge, which I did taking a plate of food and cutlery with me, the coffee table serving as temporary dining table.

She sat on an adjacent chair with her plate on her lap. "Hopefully Dr. Bedford, you won't mind talking shop while we enjoy our meal, we have a lot to talk about concerning the plans for the next few days, starting with us wanting you to meet up with Lorenzo Infanta!"

Chapter 14.

Almost choking on a potato wedge, I spluttered, "You can't be serious, Infanta will shoot me dead as soon as he sees me."

"There are several factors, Dr. Bedford that go against that statement becoming a reality. For one, we plan on setting up your meeting with him in a public place. Two, he never shoots anyone himself and we are not going to allow any of his men anywhere close to this venue and three, we are going to provide you with protective underclothing to help keep any aimed or stray bullets away from your vital organs."

Taking a deep breath I asked, "Why do I need to meet with him?"

"That Dr. Bedford is where your new tie comes into play. We will be recording both sound and vision of your conversation. We want Infanta to reveal all, especially that he is a crime gang leader and it was on his direct orders that certain crimes were committed, especially the murders."

"Do you think he'll fall for that, I mean why would he own up to me that he has done all these things?"

"Because you're going to goad him Dr. Bedford and Lorenzo Infanta won't be able to hold himself back when he's being pushed as such, he's far too proud a man to miss an opportunity to boast about his own business achievements."

"And he won't suspect that I'll be wired?"

"Oh yes of course he will, but we're going to plant a more regular recording device on you, which you're going to let him find and destroy. When he examines the actual tie itself, he won't have a clue of its capabilities, it appears to be just a normal tie after all."

I took another deep breath.

"It seems you have it all laid out, will it really be that easy?"

"You can bank on it Dr. Bedford. In fact I don't often promise anyone anything, but this I will promise you; I am one hundred percent confident that this will work and that you will be safe. Now how's the pizza?" She took a bite of hers and purred her delight at the taste. She was beginning to remind me of the character Hetty in the TV series 'NCIS - Los Angeles'!

Looking down at my plate, I thought that my rapidly changing appetite was becoming an all too regular issue.

Standing, I walked a few steps then turned to face Walsh. "What about the Badgley's, will Brunelli look after them if I reveal the safe house?"

"Please Dr. Bedford, as I've previously stressed, DON'T TELL ANYONE where that safe house is until I tell you it's safe to do so." She was very firm on this matter. "ANYONE!"

I nodded total acceptance.

"In fact we are going to leave the Badgley's safely tucked away in your safe house for a couple of days and proceed with them as you originally had planned to."

"You mean, still take Irma to visit Joe in prison on Tuesday?"

"Yes, that also is a conversation we want to record, it will help with getting Joe Badgley's conviction reviewed."

"So you don't agree with Brunelli, that he's guilty?"

"Well let's say I always had my doubts when the evidence against Tommaso Moretti suddenly started to point Joe Badgley's way. We'll go more into that matter at a later time."

I again nodded and finally took a bite of pizza while I also digested the information.

"Then what about the rest of Infanta's staff?"

"My men will take care of each and every one of them once we have located them, that's not only here in the U.K., but also all the overseas people as well. We're coordinating a synchronized arrest so that no-one will have time to warn any of the others.

"So where do we start?"

"I need that evidence first to get Lorenzo Infanta convicted. We have a briefing tomorrow at 0800, and then after all the team knows what we're doing, we wait for your evidence collecting from recording Infanta's confessions. Then if and only if everyone is in place, we spring the trap and bring them all in. That could be tomorrow or it could be later, I hope we won't keep you from your bride-to-be too much after that."

"When do I get to meet up with Infanta and where?"

"Infanta has secured management rights in a football player named Enrico Nobili, it means that the poor kid is owned by Infanta and he wants to use the boy to recruit other youngsters for criminal activities, namely match fixing, illegal gambling and maybe more people trafficking and who knows what other despicable things Infanta has in mind for those kids."

"That's back in Italy?"

"No, Nobili signed for the Arsenal Football Club only last week, tomorrow Infanta meets him off the plane to take him back to Virginia Waters presumably to work on him. This kid is famous, thousands of young boys all over Europe follow his social media pages, and those are Infanta's likely targets."

"You think maybe these youngsters could be sold to terrorist groups?" I enquired. "I'm aware many such groups get kids brainwashed and used as suicide bombers."

"We don't think any terrorist group is on Infanta's customer lists, yet. But I suppose if the right deal was offered him…. There are many other despicable potential clients he has though, for a multitude of sordid uses for the youngsters."

My blood curdled. It was going to be a real pleasure to take Lorenzo Infanta down!

❖

We spent the next hour or more discussing the tactics that I was going to use to get Infanta talking enough to incriminate himself and finishing off the pizza.

I thought several times about calling Sam back, but decided to let her at least try and get some rest.

Ms. Walsh had arranged for a room to spend the night one level up from where we talked. That's where I spent the night, exhausted from several days now without a quality sleep. That night however I slept like a log!

Next morning I was awakened by a knock on the door at 6 a.m.

"Whose there?" I called out.

"Security Dr. Bedford sir, I have some fresh clothing for you." Came the reply.

On opening the door, there stood a security guard in uniform and carrying a box. Taking the box, I thanked him and went back inside.

The box contained some underclothes made seemingly of the same material as the necktie, my protective gear no doubt.

After I'd showered and dressed, which included the new protective gear and the necktie - the room phone rang, it was Ms. Walsh.

"Good Morning Dr. Bedford. I hear you have received the little gift I sent you. Hopefully it fits comfortably."

"Good morning to you as well Ms. Walsh and yes thank you it all fits nicely, though I'm more concerned whether it will do the job or not."

"You don't have to worry Dr. Bedford, if you would like to see a demonstration we can arrange it, but rest assured this fabric has been in use now for some time and successfully tried out in the field. Have you eaten yet this morning Dr. Bedford?

"Not as yet Ms. Walsh, I'm just about to make a coffee."

"Well if you give me your order, I'll make sure the kitchen delivers it to you. It's not exactly full room service, but it will suffice for one morning I'm sure."

"No thanks, the coffee will do just fine for the moment."

"Good." Walsh paused for a moment "Dr. Bedford, there has been a slight change of plan. Young Mr. Nobili has decided to take an earlier flight. It means that you won't be attending the briefing this morning, but will be taken directly to Heathrow to meet up with Lorenzo Infanta. Senor Brunelli and I will be at the meeting with the main bulk of the team, but the people I'm sending with you Dr. Bedford are some of the very best, you will be in very capable and safe hands!"

"What time should I be ready?"

"Simon will pick you up at 8.15. With him will be Marie and Donald. They've been with me for a long time at the NCA and I promise; they will bring you back in one piece!"

"That will be fine Ms. Walsh." I confirmed, "It's good to know the National Crime Agency has my back. I need to call Sam again, will this phone connect me?"

"Yes, just dial zero, zero for the secure line out. Anything else you need in the meantime and you can get me on zero two. Good luck with Lorenzo Infanta, we all have faith in you Dr. Bedford." She hung up the phone before I could say goodbye.

I called Sam straight away. She'd had a reasonable night as the hospital had given her something to help her sleep. She and Giorgio had just arrived at the hospital with their NCB/Interpol entourage and were about to go inside the hospital foyer.

We chatted for a while as newly engaged lovers do, then I assured her of my love and safety with the coming day's events and we said our goodbyes.

Reviewing the things I was going to go through with Lorenzo Infanta, I felt solid in my conviction and of finally putting this evil man away for good. Yes he was Sam's uncle and yes he'd looked after her for the past ten years, but what he'd done in the name of self-preservation and greed just can't go unpunished. Sam and Giorgio felt the same, it was time to take him down.

Agent Simon Baxter knocked on the door at exactly 8.15. He was a tall strong looking man dressed in black slacks and the NCA's black jacket.

At the lift he used the same technique that Walsh had the previous day, I.D. tag to call the lift and retina scan and keypad to access the floor levels.

"Will I get my own retina logged on and a pass code?" I asked half-jokingly.

"Only if you come aboard with us full time Dr. Bedford." Then he smiled a knowing smile. There's a lot of perceptive people around here I thought to myself.

"Do you reckon that I will?" I asked him speculatively.

He just gave me that knowing smile again in reply!

Marie and Donald were waiting in a parked car outside when we got there, Simon introduced them.

"Just Don please, only Assistant Director Walsh still calls me Donald." Don requested as I shook his hand. The others smiled, obviously Ms. Walsh's formality with names was a bit of a team joke.

We drove off in the direction of Heathrow discussing the procedures in the Infanta entrapment plan to ensure everything went as smoothly as possible.

"We're going to try to confront Infanta before he meets up with Nobili." Simon said. "Nobili will be met by a representative of Arsenal FC and a group of journalists, before he's due to meet up with Infanta. Mr. Infanta is expected to have only Danny Weston with him as a driver. We will separate them using airport security as Mr. Weston has previous misdemeanors involving him coming in and out of the country so it will be easy to get him pulled to one side without arousing suspicion."

I nodded my understanding.

Simon continued, "Marie and Don here will do some general surveillance of the area or if any other Infanta gang member shows up, they will take them away from the scene, while I focus on discreetly looking after you as you speak to Infanta, who we'll expect to be sitting enjoying a cappuccino at The Perfectionists Café, his regular break stop when at Heathrow. All clear, Dr. Bedford?"

"Crystal, but what if he's not at the café?"

"We'll find him, it will be somewhere in that vicinity as he's booked a corner of the café so that he can have some quiet time."

"A quiet time - at Heathrow airport, I doubt it!"

"Well that might work to our advantage. The noise of a crowd in the background with airport security holding them at bay, Infanta might be more careless with his tongue as he talks to you."

We arrived at Terminal 2 and parked.

An airport security officer was there to meet us and we followed her to the security area on level one where two other security officers awaited us in an ancillary room.

"It's good to have you local airport people helping us on this one." Simon said after the introductions.

"We're always ready to help you guys from NCA." The most senior looking officer whose name was Graham, announced.

"We'll be sure to mention it in dispatches." Simon half joked. "Dr. Bedford and I will go straight to our little rendezvous point, so Don and Marie will fill you in as per our requirements."

With that Simon led the way out of the room and I followed him.

"Level five is where Infanta should be, close to 'The Perfectionists'. We will wait on level four till we get the go ahead that he definitely is there and that Danny has been sidelined by security, we don't want them to see you until Infanta is alone."

I adjusted the necktie. "Nervous? Simon enquired.

"A little, after all this is my first experience of proper detective work." I responded. "And also the fact that I'm keen to ensure this works and we get Infanta locked up good and tight."

Simon agreed. "Don't we all. No worries Dr. Bedford, sorry Joe. You'll do a great job just don't lose your cool with him!"

We stopped at Caviar House on level four for some food and drink while we waited.

It was about twenty five minutes later that Simon got the call - Infanta was seated in The Perfectionists and Danny had been picked up by security.

"Come on Joe, time to get the show on the road!" He claimed standing up.

This was it, the big moment had arrived.

Chapter 15.

A TV monitor was showing the jet that was carrying Enrico Nobili landing safely, the huddle of sports reporters waiting on the tarmac for their chance of photos and hopefully a scoop story. It could be some time before Nobili was free to meet up with Infanta.

Turning to look back at Infanta waiting for his coffee order in a secluded corner, I had to work hard not to go up to him and throttle him myself.

The blue seating in 'The Perfectionists' matching the blue of my new necktie, the necktie that was going to record all the evidence needed to put Infanta away for life.

I walked over to a young man making coffee and told them that I was Infanta's relative and wanted to surprise him by taking his coffee over. The barista OK'd it with his manager.

As I walked over to Infanta with the coffee, I drank some of it. Reaching the table I placed the half full cup in front of Infanta saying. "Thank you for visiting The Perfectionists, the coffee is delicious this morning, I know because I've just enjoyed some of yours."

Infanta's initial anger turned to surprise when he saw who had delivered his already half-empty cup. This quickly turned to a semi-smile.

"Dr. Joe Bedford. Well what a surprise. Since you've already drunk half of that one, you'd better sit and finish the rest of it." He called the waiter and re-ordered.

I sat down opposite him and moved the cup closer to my position.

"You know Joe I hear through the grapevine that we are to become almost relatives. Normally a person would congratulate a future nephew-in-law but under the circumstances I'm sure you'll forgive me if I don't. Not that you have a choice in the matter anyway since there is no way that you will survive to marry my niece! In fact by the end of this week, I will have had you, shall I say 'taken care of'!"

"You mean like you did with Marco and, how many others would it be 'uncle Lorenzo'?"

"Come now Joe, there's no need for nastiness. You and I had quite a nice bit of business going between us. I'm even hoping you're going to leave your time travel equipment to me in your will."

I was hoping to steer around the mentioning of time travel, but it was already out and recorded by whoever was monitoring the surveillance equipment.

After getting Infanta's confessions, I was going to have to come up with something to explain what Infanta was referring to.

"And what other despicable acts have you been up to, we've got murder covered, of course we mustn't forget Carlos, that is what you had planned for him also, I believe?" I quickly changed the subject of focus.

"I don't know what you're talking about. It couldn't be a little game of entrapment you are playing, eh Joseph Bedford? How naughty of you and quite naive of you to think that I would fall for your trickery."

We stopped talking when the waiter brought Infanta's second coffee over. "Would that be all for now, sir? Chef Blumenthal has just introduced some fantastic new indulgences for our special clientele."

"No thank you. We perhaps need to be left alone for the time being." I told the waiter, who bowed politely and returned to duties elsewhere.

"Take off your Jacket." Infanta demanded.

"I'm sorry, what do you mean?" I countered, playing along.

'Take it off, I want to examine your jacket."

I took my jacket off and handed it to him.

He searched all the pockets and felt around the fabric, finally satisfied he threw the jacket on the seat next to him.

Infanta stood up and walked around to my seat placing his hands around my neck as if in playful strangulation. I just sat calmly letting him go through his search for listening devices routine.

He felt through the necktie carefully and then moved onto my shirt's breast pocket where the fake device was.

"Tut, tut, tut. I am disappointed Joe." He said taking out the fake device.

Returning to his seat he deposited the device in what remained of my coffee. It bubbled and gave a slight hiss as if in a last breath of death throes.

"For such a clever man DOCTOR Bedford, you can be quite stupid sometimes. Did you think I would not check you for bugs?"

"I had to at least try."

"And who may I ask was going to be listening in to our little conversation? the police?"

Pulling out a fake business card from my back trouser pocket that was part of our setup, I handed it to Infanta to read.

"Sergeant James Heggerty, Hampshire Police. Ah, must be a friend of Papa Bedford hey Joe. You really have to aim higher you know."

The card followed the listening device into the coffee.

"But you know what old Lorenzo thinks Joe? That you are full of it! A little birdie told me that you have been talking to Interpol. Am I right eh Joe?" I didn't answer.

"And that reminds me." He leant over and firmly patted the area where the bullet had grazed my shoulder. "How is your arm? I think you were mighty lucky eh Joe. You could have been killed there and then. Of course it means that Danny will now get his wish of finishing you off himself, to repay you your kindness of almost breaking his jaw behind my garage, when you kidnapped my cook."

I refused to show any pain. "So the shooting at the hospital was your little gift Infanta, I might have known as much. An early engagement present perhaps."

Infanta started to show his true worth and began losing his cool and banging his fists down on the table and getting the brief attention of the whole restaurant.

"Listen here Bedford. Who the hell do you think you are? I'm the one calling the shots. I'm the one who worked his way up from nothing. I'm the one who did whatever I could to get to where I am today, yes head of one of the most successful crime rings in the entire world.

"My business is worth billions, something that you and your time machine will never be able to achieve. You're petty, that's what you are Joe, petty. The only good thing you've done for me is to get rid of that stupid Carlos. You've saved me from having to get Luigi do away with him so he can stay rotting in 1698 for all I care. And soon I will have you killed, yes like I had Marco killed, Carlos was too much a coward to do the job, that two timing piece of dirt. He thought he was so clever also. A cop pretending to be one of my men ha, two can play that game. I have my own infiltrator that has been keeping me in the loop all along. And even my own brother turned traitor on me, he too I had killed, had him driven off the road!"

"Massimo? You ordered Massimo, Sam's father killed?" I was beginning to boil!

"Yes, just as surely you are next Joe Bedford."

I lurched at him, grabbing him by the front of his shirt, just as Simon hastened towards us wearing an airport security uniform. "Now, now sir, we can't allow behavior like that here. You're going to have to come with me."

He handcuffed me and said to Infanta. "One of my colleagues will be along shortly to take a statement from you sir. Don't worry we'll look after this one." Infanta must have thought that one of the restaurant staff had called airport security.

Simon picked up my jacket and walked me out of The Perfectionists, the entire place gaping on at the live show presented for them.

As we walked out of Infanta's sight, Simon whispered, "Well done Joe, we got it all. Plenty there to convict him on, so good job."

We stopped around the corner so he could take the handcuffs off.

"What about Infanta? He's not going to wait to give a statement to anybody. He'll be gone in a jiffy."

"And we'll be tailing him until we're ready to arrest the entire group, remember?"

"Yes, of course. You mean we did it?"

"We've got full video and audio coverage of everything. That last one we had no idea about, having his brother killed, that alone is enough for twenty years inside."

"I'm going to have to tell Samantha and the family. That's one bit of news that's going to hit them very hard."

"Yes, but please Joe, after all the arrests. We don't want to risk anything going wrong there."

Taking a deep breath I responded "Of course. Simon, what's next on the agenda?"

"Immediately next we're heading back to HQ and debriefing."

We collected Don and Marie from nearby and returned to the car for the drive back to the Hertfordshire warehouse.

Chapter 16.

The de-briefing went smoothly. Attending were the team from the airport consisting of the three NCA officers and myself, Walsh, Dylan Burrows and one of his laboratory technicians - Stan Copeland who had been manning the recording equipment and also two legal eagles, Chief Crown Prosecutor Nadine Jamil and her assistant Colin Bainbridge of the Crown Prosecutions Service.

Each of those active in the operation discussed how things had gone from their perspective. When it came to Stan, he played back the recordings from the necktie.

I was truly amazed by the clarity achieved by this fantastic new technology, as were all who attended.

Although Nadine and Colin looked at each other and then at me when the comments about time travel came up, I just shrugged my shoulders as if I was ignorant of the matter. Fortunately for me nothing else about it was mentioned, they all seemed so pleased at how well the operation had gone and how the necktie had performed.

"What about what Infanta said about also having someone in the NCB?" I asked.

"We've been aware for some time of a mole within the NCB ranks." Walsh replied. "We know who it is and are collecting evidence there as well."

The meeting ended when the two legal participants agreed that there was plenty enough evidence to get Infanta convicted and then they and Dylan and Stan left the room.

"I must say team, a job well done. Thank you all for your efforts." Walsh praised the ones still there. "Marie and Donald you two are up for a break, please report back here at 1400 hours." At which they also left the room.

She turned to me. "Dr. Bedford, again I can't express enough thanks for your cooperation today and I want the three of us now to discuss something that you will first baulk at, but after some honest reflection on what Simon and I will tell and show you, something that you will come around to."

"Okay, you have me intrigued at least Ms. Walsh, pray continue with whatever it is you have to tell me."

She looked at Simon. "First Dr. Bedford, please come this way." Simon beckoned as he opened the door.

We walked to the lift and he swiped his I.D. tag to call the lift car.

We didn't wait for long, when the lift arrived we all went inside.

"Without telling us out loud what the number is," Simon asked me, "think of the date that your father brought home a puppy you named Gypsy when you were a boy."

I thought of the date, it was still very clear in my mind.

"OK got it." I told him.

"Now I want you to scan your retina, left eye and input that date plus 01 plus the number 27 into the keypad."

"But I haven't had my retina logged into your system, it won't recognize me." I protested.

"Please humour me Dr. Bedford."

I did as I was asked, scanned my retina and input the required numbers into the keypad. To my amazement it was all green lights and the lift started to travel downwards.

"What the… How on earth did you get my retina scanned into the system without me knowing? And that date password, what's going on, Ms. Walsh please enlighten me."

Walsh had a huge grin on her face, as did Simon. "All in good time Dr. Bedford, all in good time." She replied.

The lift door opened at what I thought to be the 27th level below ground.

We walked along the corridor, Simon leading the way until he stopped in front of a closed door with his back leaning against it.

"What you will see now Dr. Bedford will probably freak you out, so please be prepared." Walsh warned me.

"I'm ready for whatever." I informed her.

I wasn't ready! Simon moved away from the door, but he didn't open it, he just pointed to the name plate attached to it.

My eyes opened so wide that I feared my eyeballs would pop out.

I reached out and touched the plate. "I" I didn't know what to say, in fact I was as they say, speechless!

"Dr. Bedford, or should I say 'Director' Bedford, welcome to your office."

Walsh opened the door and ushered me inside the room, the plate had read 'Director Joe Bedford'.

We went in and I immediately sat down on the visitor's side of a nice walnut desk.

"Actually Dr. Bedford," Walsh pointed to the other side of the desk, "that is your seat."

Staying put, I looked around the room. If I was going to set myself up a new office, this is how I would do it; it was me in every way.

"Simon and I," Walsh explained. "Are the visitors in this office in more ways than one, we come from the future, a little over twenty years in Simon's case and I'm from a few years later, 2068 actually. In about eighteen years' time you are going to transport to the past in order to set up these premises to advance your time travel program. Then in conjunction with a newly formed world policing organization representing over two hundred nation's law enforcement agencies, you are going to be the first Director of the Chronology Crime Prevention unit, the CCP."

"Time Police!" I blurted out.

"Basically yes." Said Walsh, "but 'time police' sounds a bit comic bookish, don't you think Dr. Bedford?"

I was still dumbfounded. Simon opened a cupboard which was off to one side of the room and poured me a straight cognac which didn't even touch the sides as it slid down my throat.

Finally I was able to speak. "That explains a lot, the comments you made Simon yesterday in the lift and also some of your previous comments Ms. Walsh." I paused to look further around the room. "No photos," I exclaimed.

"No, we were unsure exactly how much to tell and show you, but your own future self has advised us to proceed with caution when it comes to divulging the most personal of details." Walsh advised. "We are still learning much on procedures and protocol in regards to time travel."

"Director Bedford?" Things still hadn't fully sunk in.

"Yes, Director Bedford/Dr. Bedford, one and the same person, just a few years different in age!" Walsh said.

"So how long have you two known me, Director Bedford I mean?"

"I've known you just the two years since you set up this department." Simon replied. "That's from the year 2046 perspective."

"And for myself," Walsh answered. "We've known each other for coming up to forty three years."

"That means in your timeline I'm in my early seventies?" I posed. And that also means I'll meet the younger you soon then?"

"All I'm going to say on that is, in your next intake of students at Cavendish, you're going to meet a Coralie Ashton. Please treat her gently and boost her first year grades beyond what you think is warranted." Walsh said with a big smile.

"Ashton, so you're married now?"

"Sorry can't say anything else."

"What about my Sam, any info you can give me there?"

Walsh moved a thumb and index finger across her closed mouth, zipped up tight!

I took a deep breath and stood up. Walking around to 'my' chair, I sat down on it to get the feel of Director Bedford.

"It feels a little too big. I guess I've put on a bit of weight in your time?"

"You could say that." Simon was still grinning.

"You're loving this, both of you aren't you!" I tried to open the desk drawers. "I suppose Director Bedford locked these so that Dr. Bedford wouldn't see what he wasn't meant to?" I was fishing. "Where is the good Director at this moment, in the building?"

"He was here yesterday when we were chatting upstairs in my office." Walsh responded. "He's gone back to 2068 to sort out a small family matter."

"I thought we couldn't travel into the future?"

"We can't. You can't travel one nanosecond beyond your current life, neither can the Director, nor anyone at the 2025 stage of time travel development."

"But it's obvious the future exists if you both are from it and are now standing in front of me in 2025. And does that mean that future progress will enable us to move forward in time?"

"We often used to think of time as a stream of water. You could swim anywhere downstream to the past or anywhere upstream to the future." Walsh explained. "The most recent thoughts are that each person's timeline is like a seagrass attached to the bank of the stream, the universal timeline. As the stream ebbs and flows, we can move upstream only as far as the extremity of the length of seagrass we are at that time. We're still anchored to the bank that is the current timeline. So unless someone can work a way to release our reed's roots from the bank so we can go further upstream….to the future beyond our own timeline! We still don't know why we can go back to any time in the universal timeline, even beyond the start of our own personal one. Director Bedford has been working on some new theories recently – 2068 recently that is, I'm sure more will be revealed eventually."

"Yes it makes sense." My mind was clicking away, but I didn't divulge any more information to the others, or they to me.

"It may make sense to you geek types, but for plain old security personnel, it's far from making sense!" Simon admitted

"Simon is that your role in the organization? You're security."

He looked at Walsh who nodded.

"Yes protective services, set up specifically to look after the future you."

"You're my body guard?"

"So to speak. Actually I'm the head of a team of your bodyguards, a team that spans the length of your life and exists in part in all the time zones from now to 2068 and beyond."

"Perhaps that is probably all we should be explaining, at least for now Dr. Bedford." Walsh interrupted. "I recall that previously you wanted out as soon as we'd acquired the evidence for convicting Infanta. Am I right in thinking that that desire may now have changed?"

I thought of my other self. I thought of the technology involved with the necktie and the establishing of the 'warehouse' we were in. I thought of Sam and our future together.

"From what you've told me, I've already agreed to stick around, from your timeline's perspective that is." I paused. "That cognac was pretty good, care to join me in another, just to celebrate my new career of course?"

"We are both still on duty Dr. Bedford, but please don't let that stop you enjoying another drink. It is after all your favourite tipple." Walsh stood up. However I'm going to ask you to retire back to your room for a few hours, so take the bottle with you and please, we are going to take you to Gatwick later so that you can pick up your vehicle, so best not to have too much, we don't want you getting a ticket for driving under the influence do we? Especially now you work for the world's leading law enforcement agency of the future."

"Do I get my set of staff keys and an I.D. tag?"

"Again all in good time Dr. Bedford, all in good time!"

That was becoming her favourite saying I think!

Chapter 17.

While waiting for the ride back to my car at Gatwick, I called Sam. Her mother's life support machine hadn't needed to be turned off, she'd died at the same time I was confronting Sam's uncle.

Deciding not to tell her over the phone that Lorenzo had given the order to have her parents killed, I instead expressed my love and told her that we'd soon be together again.

She wanted to come to me immediately, but we arranged for her and Giorgio to fly over to London on Thursday afternoon after I'd helped the Badgley's and hopefully by the time all the arrests had been made. This gave them the opportunity to start thinking about some funeral arrangements.

Simon came for me about 1.55p.m.

This time both Don and Marie were with him and we went up to the ground floor together in silence.

As the lift opened to the warehouse foyer, Simon held me back, letting the other two walk ahead.

He leant over to whisper in my ear, "These two know nothing about the time travelling. They're both completely dependable as part of your body guard team in this time period, but the Directors orders are that they shouldn't be informed concerning that aspect of our business."

"The less people know the better."

"That's exactly what the Director said!" We both smiled. It was weird but humorously weird. Of course the Director and I would be of the same mind as myself, he was me!

We entered the awaiting car, Don into the driver's position with Marie up front next to him. "I believe a big welcome to the company is due Dr. Bedford." Don said cheerfully. News travels fast in the CCP it seems.

Marie turned and smiled, "Simon said that you wouldn't be able to resist joining us, welcome aboard."

"Simon has me pretty well summed I think," I played along returning the smile to her first and then to Simon who also grinned but for the humour of the secret we shared.

As we drove to Gatwick, Simon explained that he was going to leave Don and Marie with me while he continued on to meet up with Ms. Walsh at NCA's HQ to help organize the arrests.

The other two had been given the strict orders to stick to me like glue, he told me. "Like bosom buddies!" Don called out.

"Hope you like garlic Joe, this guy can reek of curry sometimes, it's all he eats." Marie quipped

"I do not just eat curry." Don protested defending himself. "For lunch and dinner maybe, but for breakfast it's hotcakes and syrup for me."

"Gross." Marie spat the word out of her mouth. "You're going to die young Donald McPherson. Change your diet and you might just survive till you're forty."

"Are they always like this?" I asked Simon.

"No, they're only putting on a special performance as part of your welcome! Well actually they can be worse at times, just like an old married couple." Simon laughed.

"Hey boss, that's not true, you love us both, you just won't admit it." Marie said turning to face me with a huge smile on her face.

"They remind me a bit of 'Deeks and Kensi' I commented.

"Deeks and who?" They all shouted in unison.

"Never mind, you real cops wouldn't understand"

"Don't worry Joe, you are in the best of hands with these two clowns." Simon's assurance ended the banter and we continued on to the airport and my car.

In the Pajero with my two minders, I drove off first to my place to sort out fresh clothing and then onto Lyndhurst and my parents place.

We stopped for a snack break at Frimley again and I used the pre-paid phone to call Stephen Badgley to see how things were going.

Tensions were high at the Jamieson's place. The lack of contact had first given them enough worries, but when they'd heard the news and seen the reporters video playback of Infanta at The Perfectionists and me being carried away in the background by airport security while Enrico Nobili stood agape as he was about to enter the cafe, well they'd really freaked out then!

Sharon was at that moment comforting Irma, the kids had all been sent to bed early to try and keep them calm and Stephen himself had just decided to pack all their stuff into his car to hightail out of there with all his family, fearful Infanta would be onto them.

I told them to stay put and that my arrest was part of the ruse, also that I had recruits with me from the NCA and that the safe house was still the best place for them, and that we would see them in the morning.

After the call to Stephen, we talked further of the procedures for the next day or two until the arrests. After consulting their agency on the phone, Don and Marie assured me that Michael Jones was a good recruit at this point in time. I called Michael and arranged for him to meet us at Mum and Dad's place.

Arriving in Lyndhurst at about 6.40pm, Michael was already waiting outside the house.

"You made Sergeant already. Congratulations." I praised Michael as we shook hands. He was a stocky man about six inches shorter than I was and his thirty year old face quite pockmarked. "You been in the sun too much Michael?"

"Oh you noticed that I'm not quite as good looking as when you last saw me. This," he said framing his face with his hands, "is courtesy of a very nasty lady who tried to resist arrest by spraying me with acid. I was fortunate to be wearing my sunnies when she did it else the doctors said I've have been blinded."

"You've gotta take more care of yourself Michael. Dad should have taught you better than that!" I said jokingly.

"Hey now look here," Michael responded, "That father of yours is the best, can't go blaming him, it was my own silly fault." He cottoned on to my ribbing. "Ha ha, you just wait till I tell him when he gets back here that you tried to blame him!"

We all moved into the house and I spent a few minutes checking everything was safe, including the time travel equipment locked in Dad's man cave hiding place.

All was good and the three ancillary units were on full charge with the main unit reading eighty seven percent.

There was no sign of anything out of place in the house so we settled in for the night.

We ordered a meal from Indian Fusion, Don's choice! then settled down to talk to Michael while Don went into Lyndhurst to pick up the food.

First, I told him my side of the recent happenings, minus the time travel aspect, of course! Then Marie talked about the NCA side of things.

"What about what Brunelli said about Irma and Stephen?" I asked Marie and Don when he had returned with dinner.

They looked at each other. "Both Simon and Assistant Director Walsh are not on the same wavelength as Brunelli." Marie said. Walsh has asked Brunelli's superiors in S.C.I.P. to hurry up with the report he said he'd sent. Other than that, we wait for anything conclusive either way."

We explained to Michael what Brunelli had told us had happened in Manchester at Stephen Badgley's place.

"Do you think this Brunelli could be Infanta's man?" Michael asked.

"It's possible, but – Brunelli saved my life when Infanta had the hitman shoot at me at the hospital in Naples." I replied. "He's been so good, provided us with NCB people as protection in Italy and he's been helping with the case so much."

"Well either Brunelli's lying or the Badgley's are." Michael reasoned. "We're going to have to tread very carefully in handling the Badgley's until we find out for sure."

"We've talked about it before, Marie and I that is." Don said stuffing his face with vindaloo. "We both trust Walsh and Simon more than we trust Brunelli, we've only just come across him and we've known the other two for years. Simon in particular doesn't do many wrong calls and Assistant Director Walsh - you don't get to her position without usually getting it right!"

I tended to agree with them, especially since both Simon and Walsh were on the time travel team as well. So I've either misread Brunelli or I've misread the Badgleys! I sure hope Sam's a better judge of character than I am!

Finishing the meal we then played cribbage as we continued our discussion. Typical English! We had some heavy duty decisions and action going down tomorrow and here we were playing cards.

It reminded me of the scene in H.G. Wells' 'War of the Worlds' when the Journalist and the Infantryman played cards while the earth was being destroyed by aliens.

"That's fifteen two, fifteen four, two's six and six is twelve, plus one for his nob, thirteen and game one to me." Marie claimed victory in the first game.

"You kept looking at my hand." Don challenged her.

"We go all the way to the finish post and then you claim I cheated. You just don't like getting beaten all the time do you sunshine." She ruffled Don's light brown hair. They started to play wrestle.

"Hey not in my parents place you don't. I'll get the blame for any breakages." I looked at Michael, "Simon warned me about these two. He was right, a pair of clowns!"

Don and Marie settled.

"You're no fun Joe Bedford. Come on I'm going to win the next game, you'll see." Don gathered up the cards, while a smiling Michael re-set the crib board.

It was then I realized it was good they were like this. The job they did was extremely stressful - I needed to relax a bit. We all needed to relax a bit!

Yes another big day tomorrow. Who will be revealed as Infanta's inside man? Will Irma Badgley prove to be Brunelli's mafia queen? All will be revealed.

Chapter 18.

The sound of breaking glass woke me. It was still dark outside, so early morning I guessed.

I rushed some track pants on and moved quietly to the bedroom door and cautiously opened it.

Don was also just coming out of his room, with a gun in hand and he held a finger to his lips encouraging my silence.

As we moved towards the top of the landing, we could just make out Marie's form slumped awkwardly on the floor downstairs not moving.

Slowly we moved downstairs, trying to watch all around us for the attacker.

Half way down, Don suggested that I return upstairs for safety's sake, but I wasn't going to be put off that easily. Besides, Marie was going to need some help - if she was still alive that is!

There was a loud bang as a gun was fired in our direction, missing both of us in the dark.

Whoever fired that shot mustn't have realized that gun flash would reveal their whereabouts in the dark and Don fired five rounds in the general direction of the flash.

There was a groaning sound and someone fell to the floor.

Don shifted to reach for the lights and then went to inspect the fallen shooter to ensure all was safe, while I rushed to Marie just as she started to come round, a bloody mat of hair evidence of where she'd been hit with the assailant's gun butt.

"You call that keeping watch!" Don jibed.

"Oh yeah, thanks Don I'm not quite dead, but I will survive with my cracked skull."

He came over to where we both knelt on the floor. Smiling he told her in the warmest softest manner which belied his actual words. "That's good - I didn't want to have to break in yet another new partner!"

She hit him hard in the chest with a clenched fist, but fell forward almost in a faint with making the effort.

Catching her before she hit the other side of her head, I helped her stand and escorted her to the couch. "Better get that looked at. The nearest surgery will be closed now, but as soon as it gets light… in the meantime let's get it cleaned up."

Don came from examining the attacker. "That one won't be doing any more harm. I think you might know him Joe, it's one of Infanta's close associates, Sebastian Theolini."

I walked over to where the body lay, three wounds evident from Don's shooting, plus a huge bruise on his chin still from where I had hit him behind Infanta's garage.

"Yes," I acknowledged to Don. "He was usually on guard duty in front of the Infanta house. Do you think he was alone?"

"You take care of Marie while I go and check around the property, better to be safe than sorry." Then he added, "I'll call Sergeant Jones as well. He won't thank me for waking him so early, but I'm sure he'll come around to seeing the need for reinforcements."

Don returned after about five minutes reconnaissance with the all clear. Just minutes later Michael turned up with four other uniformed constables, two of which moved Sebastian's body to the wood shed after taking photos and bagging him.

Michael had more first aid training than any of us and suggested one of his men take Marie straight to Southampton's University Hospital for treatment. She protested loudly, but after nearly collapsing again, acceded to Michael's counsel and was taken by one of his officers.

"What about the Badgley's?" Don enquired, "Shouldn't we check on them."

"There's no way Infanta could know where they're hiding out." I suggested. "I'm the only one who knows, even Walsh and Simon don't know where the safe house is."

"Best leave them, we don't know if anyone else is still watching us here and if you go to the safe house, you could be followed." Michael decided for us. "Joe, what time are you taking Irma Badgley up to Manchester?" He asked.

"The visit is scheduled for 2.00p.m., with Joe Badgley in Strangeways. I was planning on leaving about seven." I looked at my watch. "Only a little less than three hours from now."

"Don, can you recruit any more NCA people to help us out, with the five of us here now, Hampshire Police will be a bit thin on the ground if we get more of our people?"

"More budget cuts hey? I'll phone it in. I'm sure we can spare a few more before we actually action operation 'Count Your Chickens'" Don replied

"Operation 'Count Your Chickens'!" I was a little incredulous at the name.

"That's what Walsh called the Infanta gang arrest operation. Don't look at me, I offered 'Operation Spaghetti Western'. She preferred 'Count Your Chickens', I just couldn't understand it neither!" Don said as if he'd been personally wounded by the decision and supposing that his choice was infinitely better!

Michael and I looked at each other and rolled our eyes. NCA officers obviously had to have a certain special mentality to get employed by the department!

"Why don't you two go and get a bit of shut eye." Michael suggested to Don and me. "We'll keep a watch down here and I can wake you both just before six o'clock, we should have news from Don's office by then about some backup. How does that sound?"

It was a good idea. I don't know if either of us was going to get back to sleep, but it wouldn't hurt to try.

I didn't even try to sleep however; instead I sat in my room and sent a text to Sam. It all too soon became light outside and after showering and donning some clean clothes on top of my protective gear, I went to put some coffee on.

Michael and Don were talking in the lounge and came into the kitchen when they heard me.

They both looked shattered from lack of sleep. "Have you heard from your office, Don?" I asked.

Yes, we'll have an extra two officers joining us any time soon. They'll drive with you to Strangeways and Simon and Assistant Director Walsh are flying up to Manchester to meet up with you there. The instructions from Simon are to go alone to pick up Irma Badgley and ensure the others stay put in the safe house for another day or two."

'Until 'Operation Count Your Chickens' is over I guess."

"Probably." Don walked over and poured himself a coffee.

"Make mine black." Called out Marie as she walked in from the rear boot room.

We all greeted her warmly, commenting on her 'hospital turban'. "That suits you. Want tandoori for breakfast?" Was Don's quip pointing to her wound dressing.

"You watch yourself McPherson." She warned jestingly. "The hospital said I wouldn't be able to go ten rounds with Daniel Dubois until next week, but they didn't mention anything about not knocking you out cold today!"

They hugged each other, then she cuffed him on the jaw playfully.

"Looks like you need a bit of sweetening, I'll put a couple of teaspoons of sugar in as well!" Don finished the exchange on top and poured her a coffee, without the sugar.

"What was the doctor's verdict?" I asked Marie.

"A couple of stitches for the cut and concussion, requiring a couple of days rest."

"So why are you back here?"

"I'll take a couple of days off - no problem, sometime later in the year maybe!"

Don shook his head. "See what I have to put up with!" He dodged another swipe from Marie.

I went off in the Pajero to get Irma, taking a different route again and brought her back to Lyndhurst where the two new NCA officers were waiting.

"This is Detective Constable Paul Applegate and Detective Constable Leroy Brown." Don introduced them.

"Bad, bad Leroy Brown," Marie began to sing.

"Leave it out Marie," He told her.

I looked at Michael. "My kids are just the same," He laughed. "You have to be Joe to get through some of the days us law enforcement types have to go through."

"Thanks Sarg." Marie said sticking her tongue out at Leroy.

I shook my head. "Don't worry Irma, These guys are A-Teamers really. They'll take good care of us."

She smiled, not looking too convinced.

"Let's get on the road, kids." I said. "Don't want to be late seeing Irma's hubby in Strangeways." I turned to the two new back-ups, "You guys were filled in about what's on today?" I asked.

They both acknowledged full awareness and offered Irma a protective vest, which she put on hurriedly as she looked in Marie's direction.

"Sorry no hard hats." Marie said and then immediately regretted it as she saw the worried look back with intensity on Irma's face.

"Come on." I said. "I'm driving."

We left, letting Michael lock up my parents place once everyone else had gone on their way and the coroner had picked up Sebastian's body.

As we drove through Lyndurst heading for the M27 and the road north, Irma, sitting up front with me, put her hand on my arm. I looked around to see her take in a deep breath. I knew exactly what this meeting with her Joe might mean to her and the whole family.

I smiled at her as if to say, 'this is all going to work out fine.' I surely hoped so!

The drive to Manchester was uneventful.

Meeting Walsh and Simon outside Strangeways Prison, Applegate and Brown stayed outside while the four of us went inside the prison.

Chapter 19.

Joe Badgley was sitting at a small refectory style table in the prison visitor room by himself when the tannoy called out his name and prison I.D. number. "Badgley 110269D, return to the visitor room pre-holding area immediately. Repeat, Badgley 110269D, return to the visitor room pre-holding area immediately."

Joe looked around in surprise.

The warder at the door of the visitor room on the prisoner's side beckoned him over.

"That's you Badgley. Don't keep the guvnor waiting now." He called out.

Joe rose from his chair and walked to the prison warder who'd spoken to him. "What's going on Mr. Stevens?" he asked.

"You tell me, Senior Chief Garcia wants to see you and your visitors in his office it seems." Stevens said unlocking the door to allow Badgley through.

Badgley was escorted by another prison officer to the Senior Chief's office, who on arriving knocked on the door and waited.

"Enter." Came the call.

The warder opened the door and prodded Badgley into the room. "Prisoner Joe Badgley 110269D reporting as ordered Sir." The warder announced.

Badgley saw Irma and moved closer to her. "Irma, what's going on?"

"Back in line prisoner." The warder grabbed Joe Badgley's shoulder and pulled him back.

"At ease Officer Vardy." Senior Chief Garcia ordered. "Vardy you can leave us now. Please wait outside to take Badgley back to his cell when we've finished."

"Yes Sir." The warder left the room closing the door behind him.

Garcia waved the ok for Irma to greet her husband. They hugged for a few seconds before Walsh interrupted.

"Mr. Badgley, Irma, please take a seat. My name is Assistant Director Coralie Walsh of the NCA Investigations division, this is Detective Senior Sergeant Simon Baxter from my office and Dr. Joe Bedford who's been helping Irma with a few problems she's had. Of course you already know the prison's Senior Chief Garcia."

Badgley looked at Irma, "Problems?" he asked, then not waiting for an answer to that question he turned to face Garcia, "What's going on Mr. Garcia?"

"I'll leave you to talk Assistant Director." Garcia said to Walsh. "Please use my chair."

"Thank you Senior Chief." Walsh thanked him as he went out of the room.

With Walsh taking the lead, we told Badgley about things that had happened up to my getting Irma out of the Infanta mansion. We didn't include information about the time travelling or Operation Count Your Chickens. Yes I cringed at the name again as well. Every time I hear it!

Badgley was visibly relieved to hear that Stephen, Sharon and the three grandchildren were safely tucked away somewhere.

"Mr. Badgley." Walsh said, getting Badgley's attention. "We are going to re-open your file. But we're going to need your help to re-testify. Joe, you were convicted of the murder of Carmel and Andrew Sabakovski. Did you really pull the trigger as you admitted in court?"

Badgley bowed his head and gently shook it, "No." he mumbled

"Tell us Joe, what happened? Do you know who did the killings?" Simon asked.

"I can't say anything. They will kill us all, Stephen, Sharon, the children." He shook his head again.

"Joe, look at me." Irma said firmly to her husband. "We can trust these people fully. They will protect us all. Infanta and all his men are going down for all their badness. We will be safe, please tell them everything." She pleaded.

Badgley looked at each one of us in turn as if assessing Irma's claimed reliance.

"Tommaso Moretti. He did the killings. I drove him to the courthouse where the coroner's hearing was scheduled to discuss the Sabakovski's son's death.

"After the postponement, we followed them back home. I waited in the car while Moretti went into the house after them. When he returned to the car, he ordered me to drive to the canal at Vicars Hall Lane Bridge outside Worsley. As we drove he emptied his gun, wiped it clean and then threw it into the canal from the bridge as we drove over."

"That was Vicars Hall Lane Bridge, outside Worsley, Manchester?" Simon asked checking the details as he took down notes.

"Yes." Badgley confirmed, "It's up near 'Lower Green' near where Stephen got his first job after school, you remember Irma?"

"Yes dear, Mr. Baxter will find it. Do you think the gun will still be there Mr. Baxter?" She enquired of Simon.

"There's no reason why it shouldn't be Mrs. Badgley. We'll get someone out there to go fishing for it as soon as we've finished here." Simon reassured her.

Badgley continued to offer more information concerning other crimes he had witnessed Moretti commit, with Simon ensuring he wrote down everything in his notebook. We both forgot that I was wearing the tie and the discussion was being recorded back at HQ by Stan.

He also mentioned the details concerning the threats to his family's lives if he didn't take the rap for the Sabakovski murders so that Moretti could escape to Italy to continue with Infanta's dirty work there.

Simon had Joe Badgley read the notes he had taken and to sign that they were the correct details.

In summing up, Walsh couldn't offer any promises concerning the reversal of the conviction. "It all depends on collecting enough solid evidence."

She advised the Badgleys. What you've given us today will really help though."

Simon again offered immediate follow up of all the new information and supported Walsh's statement by adding, "We'll do all we can, Joe."

As Simon went to get Officer Vardy from waiting outside and Joe and Irma said their goodbyes, I leant over to Walsh and quietly asked, "Do we get his conviction reversed? You already know the future."

"I know the full outcome Dr. Bedford, as long as the timeline isn't changed somehow. Up to 2068, we are not aware of any other timelines developing. However, as we've already mentioned, your future self, Director Bedford, has given us full instructions NOT to tell you details that are only part of our history and are yet for your future. So I'm sorry, but you will have to wait until events happen to find out the details."

I huffed a curse at my future self – wait till I have a word with him!

It was three forty by the time we signed out of the prison.

Applegate and Brown had waited patiently outside for us and we drove to Interpol's new UK headquarters near Deansgate.

There Applegate and Brown took Irma to an interview room to rest up and get them all some refreshments.

With Walsh leading the way, she, Simon and I walked through the extensive building towards the 'operations control room'. As we went, several of the staff saw Simon and spoke to him, "Congratulations Senior Sergeant.' One said. "Simon Baxter, good to see you again said another." "What's this new secret assignment, Simon?" Asked another.

"Like its secret Joyce. No can tell, sorry." He replied.

"I thought it's another 18 years before you join up Simon?" I queried discreetly.

"That's for the warehouse project, the CCP." He told me, "But for this time zone, I've worked from this office for about twenty months now. It helps me in looking after Director Bedford's needs in whichever time zone he's in and I can act as a go-between updating those in my time zone and those from the future who've come back in time, like Miss Walsh here."

"Doesn't it get confusing?" I asked

"Not really. One of the Director's rules is that we can't appear in too many time zones, especially those periods that are close to one another."

"So you don't keep on running into your other self?"

"Yes and so that your colleagues don't get confused." Walsh added

"What would you or the good Director say was the most difficult or dangerous aspect of travelling to and fro in time?"

Walsh and Simon stopped. Ensuring no one was listening Walsh said, "New time travelers asking too many questions!"

"And getting older faster than everyone else in your own time zone." Simon rescued me smiling.

"Yes of course." I exclaimed in a lightbulb moment. "If you spend too much time in a different time zone, when you return to you own time, you've aged all the time you have spent away, while those in your time zone have just aged normally!"

"So another of Director Bedford's rules is, 'no more than one week away from your own time zone at any one time. And another is no more than one month in total spent away from your own time zone each year." Walsh said

"It seems the future me has more rules than Gibbs does!"

"Sorry," Simon said confused.

"NCIS Special Agent Gibbs, oh never mind."

We continued to the operations control room without any more talking.

Chapter 20.

We walked into an ongoing conversation between two men sitting at a boardroom table and another younger man standing and giving an explanation of something on a whiteboard.

I had to look twice at the man standing and turned to Walsh for confirmation, looking at her questioningly.

She nodded confirmation of my thoughts. The young man was a younger version of Dylan Burrows, the Physics specialist at the warehouse. This version wasn't in a wheelchair though, but very active on his feet and very animated at his presentation.

"You don't know each other yet, Dr. Bedford, so please keep mum. All will be revealed in due time." Walsh whispered.

The younger Burrows finished his presentation with, "Well what do you think gentlemen, worth a try?"

"Definitely." Declared one of the seated officers, "Caleb, are you seeing what I'm seeing here? The potential is enormous in getting a response team out to where they're needed, cutting delays in getting to a crime scene considerably. It'll really help our conversion rates."

The one addressed as Caleb nodded. "Well done Burrows. You've been with us, what three weeks is it now and you're already proving you've got what it takes." He looked around at us. "We'll trial it next week. You two get together on Monday and sort it out. That will be all for now Burrows, we have some pressing things to discuss with Assistant Director Walsh, keep up the good work."

Burrows gave a big grin. "Thank you Chief Superintendent, Senior Field Agent Perera." He nodded to both and took his leave, nervously twitching as he passed Walsh on the way out, but still smiling.

"Seems like a happy and capable young man Caleb, Burrows you called him?" Walsh commented.

"Yes, Dylan Burrows. We picked him up from private industry, he wanted to do more for his fellow human beings than just line the pockets of the shareholders. Could have accepted a position with NASA but chose us instead."

"He's helping our field agents at the present set up a new communication system that he's developed in the short time he's been here." Perera said. "I think the boy will go places!"

"Assistant Director Walsh, you remember Senior Field Agent Darsh Perera, I'm sure. Simon, good to see you again and well done on the promotion."

"Good to see you again too Sir, and may I take the opportunity to thank you, I believe it was your word that swayed the promotions board."

"A little bird it was that whispered into my ear about a very capable young Sergeant Baxter." He winked at Walsh, his Irish accent becoming more noticeable.

"Well thank you both then. Hello Darsh, looks like you're on the up as well." Simon shook hands with Perera. "This is Dr. Joe Bedford." He introduced me.

"Ah Dr. Bedford." Caleb Howarth said as he held out his hand. "I believe we really have to thank you most of all."

"I don't know about that Chief Superintendent." I said not knowing what he was referring to but accepted the handshake.

"Without you, Dr. Bedford." Walsh came in, "We wouldn't be anywhere near as ready to make the arrests we're about to make. It's your help that's going to enable us to put a complete end to Infanta's activities!"

"I think anyone in my position would do the same to stop such heinous crimes, I'm just doing what I can."

"No Dr. Bedford, credit where credit is due. You were the one who managed to get Infanta talking, you were the one who put his life on the line."

"Ms. Walsh you told me that I wasn't in danger, that you had all bases covered."

"I did, didn't I!" Walsh spoke with a grin, "But what I didn't mention is that sometimes things do go wrong, not according to plan that is. Like last year in a similar operation, you remember Simon, we lost a new recruit who was shot trying to corner Infanta into admitting one of his crimes."

"Now you tell me, thanks very much."

All the others broke out into laughter then someone else entered the room.

"Assistant Director Walsh Ma'am, Chief Superintendent we have just received a call from the Milan office." The newcomer handed Howarth a sheet of paper and then exited the room again.

We all sat down as we waited for Howarth to read the report.

"Good news and bad news," He started holding the report sheet up in front of us. "This highlights Dr. Bedford how things can suddenly switch to going wrong, just when you think you're on a winner." He took a deep breath in.

"It's Brunelli reporting from Milan; 'Matteo Lombardi,'" he scanned from the report. "The hit man who shot at you Dr. Bedford was being tailed after leaving Naples. Well he twigged that he was being followed and pulled a gun on Brunelli and the other three NCB officers on the job with him. In the encounter one of Brunelli's men turned and killed another member of the team and then tried to kill Brunelli himself. Brunelli it seems was too quick and killed Infanta's infiltrator while the other loyal officer killed Lombardi."

Everyone felt saddened by the loss of the loyal law enforcement agent.

"But now I really am confused." I stated scratching my head. "If that dead NCB officer was Infanta's infiltrator and Brunelli isn't, then what about the things he said concerning the Badgley's? Does that mean Irma and Stephen Badgley **are** crime figures as bad as Infanta himself? None of it makes any sense!"

Simon explained to the others what I was talking about, the story Brunelli had told us about the Badgleys.

"I think the best we can do is to keep an eye on the Badgley's until we know for sure." Walsh instructed. "Dr. Bedford, I think it's time for you to reveal your safe house and then we pick up all the Badgleys and take them to a new location where we can keep a close watch on them. Caleb I want you to take charge of that little operation straight away. Get a competent PC with Irma Badgley right now and get all the Badgley's together at wherever that location is. Simon, you go back with Joe and take Applegate and Brown with you. The Chief Superintendent and I will teleconference with the various countries heads of department involved in Operation Count Your Chickens and work out a 'go' time."

Everyone paused for it all to sink in.

"Come on jump to it, Dr. Bedford the address please." She picked up a pen and pad from off the table and handed it to me. "Caleb a word in your ear if you will."

Moving to one side with Howarth, she conferred with him while I wrote down the Jamieson's address and handed it to Perera as he was on his mobile phone arranging someone to look after Irma.

"Simon, Dr. Bedford, with me. Caleb I'll just brief these two and then return for our conference call."

Walsh exited the room waving us to follow to a small adjacent office.

Closing the door when we had all entered, she looked focused and said. "I want you two to be extra careful. Until we know precisely who we're dealing with as adversaries, trust only each other and those I directly assign to be with you."

"Again, why can't we use your future knowledge to ensure our safety?"

"Because Dr. Bedford,"

"The future Director Bedford ordered it that way." Walsh and I said that last sentence together.

"The best we can do Joe," Simon explained, "Is to follow along exactly as recorded in our future files. That way we minimize the risk of changing the timeline."

"Has it ever worked out differently to what is noted in the future records?" I asked.

"Not that we know at this point in time or rather even from Ms. Walsh's point in time in 2068."

"I think this could drive me crazy!"

"You're not the first to think that about yourself Dr. Bedford." Walsh said with a big grin.

"Don't worry Joe, I think you'll get her back one day."

"Believe me Simon. I'm working on a plan to do just that right now!"

We all smiled.

"What about Brunelli? Can we clear him of any underhand dealings?" I asked

"We'll treat Senor Brunelli with the same wariness as the Badgley's for now. I know the outcomes of the operation, but I have to keep things to myself, as does Simon. None of us may be happy with all of the outcomes as per the record books, but that's what we have to accept."

I chewed things over in my mind for a moment. There were obviously things going to happen that we/I wouldn't be fully content with. I had to accept that.

"Come on Simon, let's find Applegate and Brown and get back to Lyndhurst. We can pick up a takeaway to eat on the way, as long as no one messes up my Pajero!"

Chapter 21

It was almost 10.00 p.m. by the time we drove into my parent's driveway. We were all tired.

I'd spoken to Sam enroute, Applegate had snored like an old man while asleep on the back seat and Simon and I had got to know each other better, talking about our pasts and what led us to settle on our current fields of work.

With both of us up front and Applegate snoring away while Brown also dozed, I had also quietly told Simon about Carlos.

When we walked into my parents place, Simon told the other two to get some rest and that we would keep first watch.

He then encouraged me outside for a security check!

"Joe, we can go and get Carlos now, he might be useful to Operation Count Your Chickens."

"But can we trust him? You know what Walsh ordered."

"Yes, but I have a gut feeling that it will be okay. Especially when we tell him that Infanta was going either kill him or leave him back in 1698."

"You're not breaking one of Director Bedford's rules are you?" I jested.

"Only the one he specifically told me to break and when to break it!"

"No way!" I exclaimed "I, the future me that is, told you that we should go and get Carlos back from 1698 - at this particular point in time?"

"Well not in so many words. What he said was that when you feel like telling me about Carlos, that's the time he should be brought back to today. He also told me to give you this." He handed me a plain white envelope from his inside jacket pocket.

I opened it and moved beneath an outdoor security light to enable me to read the information it contained.

"What does it say?" Simon enquired.

"It's machine code. Hold on, it's quite complex."

I nodded several times as I it dawned on me what the information was going to help with as regards the main time travel unit.

"It's an adjustment to the time travel programme." I told Simon. "Up until now, I've only been able to travel forward to the very limit of the second of travelling backwards. For example, if I leave now to go back in time, I can only come back to the moment I left and no further I.E. to this point in time. This formula means that whatever normal time has elapsed since I returned from 1698 can also be added onto Carlos's return time."

"I don't understand what you're saying." Simon admitted

"Don't worry, I'm struggling myself to see how it works. I think it depends on the longevity of the time travel units, especially the transmitter. With the current programme, Carlos can only return to the point when we originally left to go to 1698, his life hasn't as yet extended beyond that time. The time travel units returned with me, so they've experienced an extended existence period. Because we'll use the same particular units to retrieve him from 1698, which exist in this timeline up to the point of whenever I go back again, we can, with this programme adjustment, bring Carlos right to that point we leave to get him back, or more precisely the point that the time travel units leave to go and retrieve him."

"Clear as mud!"

I started to think out loud as we walked around the property having picked up a couple of flashlights.

"It's best if I go alone," I told Simon, "we'd have enough power in the units, but also Carlos might not welcome the idea of an NCA Senior Sergeant coming with me to rescue him. And I should return to somewhere we could be alone so I can explain to him that Infanta wanted him dead and feed him with the idea that the NCA are going to be his friends."

"Where would you take him?"

I thought for a moment. "Back to the Infanta house in Virginia Water so he could overhear what Infanta and Luigi were talking about - killing the both of us."

"No, that sounds too risky." Simon warned, "What if we set up a video of your conversation with Infanta at 'The Perfectionists'? Infanta clearly talks about his despise of Carlos in that and his plans to do away with him."

"Great idea, but how can we get hold of a copy of the video, isn't it with Walsh for her to give as part of the prosecution evidence?"

"I have a copy on my phone, she sent it me while we were driving from Manchester." Simon smiled at the look on my face.

"You've both been playing this all along haven't you, pulling the strings? You know exactly what's going to happen and when it's going to happen."

"Honestly Joe, all we're doing is following the report as it was archived in Walsh's time. That says that you brought Carlos back here to Lyndurst first while it was empty with us being in Manchester, and that when you finally get to the here and now, you play the video for Carlos. I think you'll find the video downloaded on the T.V.'s hard drive already when you get back. After you show Carlos the video and tell him about NCA involvement, that's the time I come out of hiding and offer him a deal for turning King's evidence." He smiled again.

"All we are doing is following a damn script! Will it always go as per the report?" I was getting frustrated and angry.

"We still have to be careful. There are a lot of unknowns still with changing the timeline possibilities. Even in the older Coralie Walsh's time of 2068, both you and Coralie, along with your science team, are still trying to find answers to some seriously huge questions concerning time travel."

I looked away from Simon, not seeing anything in particular, just staring into thin air! I shook my head. "You know Simon it's very tempting for me to go back in time and visit my younger self and plead with him to stick with martial arts and forget going into physics!"

"The trouble with that Joe is that if you don't invent your time travel gear, Infanta won't get stopped and put away."

After a couple of really deep breaths, I turned back to Simon. "Well I better go and get Carlos back from 1698 then. You coming to upload that video?"

We headed off towards dad's man cave to retrieve the time travel units. Looks like I was going to play along at the current timeline's game after all!

Chapter 22.

Simon checked on Applegate and Brown. Brown was asleep upstairs while Applegate had crashed on the couch in the lounge. Simon gave him a shake, "Applegate, go on up to one of the bedrooms for a sleep, Dr. Bedford and I need to discuss a few things down here and we'll only keep you awake."

"Sure thing Sarg." He stretched then slowly got up and went upstairs.

I popped my head around the door to check the coast was clear and brought in the time travel units, two at a time. I also brought the guns that I had acquired, one from the wine cellar and also Danny and Sebastian's guns from the fight behind the garage. I offered them all to Simon, explaining where they had come from.

"Here take one back." He held out one of the guns to me. "You might need it at the palace with those guards."

"No thanks, I can't risk killing anyone who escapes the fire and changing the timeline."

Simon just smiled at me.

"I suppose it's in 'the report' that I take a gun."

He nodded. "But I can't say any more than that."

I took the gun and tucked it into the back of my trouser belt.

"Where will you hide?" I asked him.

"At the top of the stairs, out of sight but where I can ensure Applegate and Brown don't come and disturb you and Carlos until you've convinced him that we're basically on his side."

"All good. You upload the video while I set the time travel units in place and programme the co-ordinates."

Simon pulled his phone out of his pocket and went and turned on the TV. I showed him where he could find a cable to connect his phone to the TV's hard drive

Positioning the four time travel units, I then set the co-ordinates to arrive in 1698 just two seconds after I'd left previously. The speed dial was set for returning to this very same spot during the time we were away in Manchester.

Then I remembered that I hadn't re-programmed the main unit with Director Bedford's changes.

I fetched my laptop and connected it to the main unit. Simon joined me - having finished at the TV, watching as I keyed in the programme changes from the piece of paper that was in the envelope.

It seemed to take forever, well about twenty minutes anyway! Simon waited patiently for me to finish, staying silent so that I could concentrate.

When I'd completed the programming he asked me, "Will it need to be tested before it's used with you as the guinea pig?"

"I think we have to trust the good Director. I've checked over the input of the programme, but really the only way to test it is to use it in the field. That is - when I go back to get Carlos. 'The report' does say that I get back doesn't it?"

Smiling again, Simon nodded. "You're pushing the boundaries again Joe. I'm going to have to add it to my own personal report to the Director!" He openly laughed now.

"Get upstairs and hide." I jokingly commanded. "Carlos and I will be back here in five seconds your time."

Simon moved away from the time units as I stepped into the travel field area. I watched him as he started upstairs then pressed the 'go' switch. He turned to say something just as I disappeared back to 1698.

Robert Burns wrote, 'The best-laid plans of mice and men often go awry'.

Well this was one of those times!

As I materialized next to Carlos in 1698, he had been getting ready to defend himself from the oncoming palace guards.

My appearance startled him and he tripped backwards and knocked over one of the ancillary time travel units, leaving us without the quick planned escape back to my parents place!

The guards had only about thirty metres to walk before they reached where we were located in the banquet hall.

Fortunately for us, my sudden appearance startled them as much as it had startled Carlos and the guard in the rear collided into the leading one, the captain, sending them both to the floor. As they fell, their swords dropped from their hands and went sliding out of reach.

If it wasn't for the seriousness of the situation, I would have laughed at the slapstick, comedy of errors that it all must have looked like.

Quickly I ran to confiscate the two lost swords and stood watch over the guards while Carlos recovered.

Carlos speedily came to my side and I handed him one of the swords.

The guards were still stunned. Then I realized that I still sported twenty first century clothing. That with my sudden appearance and that of the time travel equipment had them dumbfounded, even fearful.

With my newly acquired sword pointed directly at the captain, I signaled the two guards to get to their feet which they tentatively obeyed.

Walking them over to the side wall of the banquet room, I had them then sit on the floor with their hands behind their backs.

"What do we do now Joe?" Carlos asked

"We set up the equipment again and hightail it out of here. You keep an eye on them while I re-position and check the equipment." I told him. "Don't let them move an inch."

Looking to the two on the floor I commanded them, "Thy being shalt be considered mere dung should ye moveth but one inch."

Carlos looked at me curiously.

I shrugged. "Sounded good to me." Then I instructed him "If they moveth an inch, run them through." Carlos seemed somewhat mystified, but I had no doubt that the two guards knew exactly what I meant and their body language showed it.

Inspecting the fallen time travel unit, I saw a small dent in the casing, otherwise the exterior seemed ok. The interior workings however were a different matter. The quantum duality emissions emanating from the main unit are sent to the receivers in the ancillary units. The ability to reflect those emissions depends immeasurably on the exact positioning and immaculate condition of the surface materials within the receivers contained within the ancillary units.

Or to put it simply, there was no way of knowing if the unit's reflector had been altered or broken by the fall without taking it to my lab and opening it up. The slightest damage internally would mean that nothing would happen when the main units function was triggered. We wouldn't be able to travel a single nanosecond or millimeter. It seemed we were now *both* stuck in 1698!

Chapter 23.

My mind began to wander, would I see Sam again? Would we end up in The Tower? No, snap out of it Joe Bedford, I told myself - I've got to think clearly.

Just as I started to re-focus, two more guards rushed into the banquet hall. These both carried muskets with bayonets attached!

As they approached, I remembered the gun and pulled it out of my belt and fired a shot towards the newcomers intentionally missing them, the bullet ending up somewhere near the door they'd entered from.

"Joe, what the hell's going on? Get the time travel gear ready. Let's get going." Carlos was starting to look a little panicky.

The gunshot noise also seemed to have stunned all the guards into extreme caution.

"What s'rt of game doth thee playeth oh strange one? And thy pistol, from wh're doest t cometh from?" The captain asked, starting to get a bit bolder.

"Silence!" I commanded the captain, and then told the two standing guards. "Thee two moveth ov'r with the oth'rs."

"My god I must dreaming I'm in a Shakespearean play or something. Joe – *please* get us out of here!" Carlos was getting quite upset.

"I don't know if we can get out." I regretted saying it as soon as the words came from my mouth.

Carlos screamed something unintelligible.

"Carlos." I shouted "Get a hold of yourself man. We're only going to get away from all this if we keep our wits about us. There's a good possibility that one of the units is damaged and can't be used. But before we even try to fix it and disappear in front of these four, we have to tie them up and blindfold them or something."

Turning to the captain, I asked, "Thee Captain, what lockable vacant cubiculos art locat'd nearby?"

"Wherefore doth thee require such knowledge?" he replied

"Answ'r the questioneth and stand ho answ'ring backeth," I shouted at him angrily. Schoolboy Shakespearean English was coming in useful after all!

He pointed gingerly towards the door opposite from which they had entered.

"The L'rd Keepeth'r's cubiculo is presently exsufflicate." He replied.

"On thy feet all of thee." I motioned for them to move to the door way.

Carlos had picked up the two muskets and had one trained towards our 'prisoners'. The other one he had swung over his shoulder as he took up the rear at a safe distance.

Taking the lead as we walked towards the indicated door, I commanded them to stop while I peered out through it to check all was clear.

Moving slowly out through the door I beckoned the captain to come through and for the others to stay put.

"The L'rd Keepeth'rs cubiculo?" I enquired of the captain.

He pointed to an adjacent door and I moved him forward towards it, encouraging him with the sword.

With one eye on the captain while holding him to a distance with the sword, I put the gun back into my belt and reached to open the Lord Keeper's door.

It was his time to take advantage of my distraction and he knocked the sword out of my hand with a deft twist and turn of his body so that he grabbed my arm at the same time and brought his knee up and planted it firmly into my solar plexus.

I was momentary stunned, if it wasn't for my martial arts background, he would have had me, but he didn't fully connect.

Using his momentum against him, I twisted with him and then brought my free hand forward to wrestle his arm around his back for a hammerlock. Thanks for teaching me that one dad!

As I held him, there was a commotion back in the banquet hall. Shouting, a pained scream, some scuffling noises and more shouting.

I quickly maneuvered the captain back so I could have vision of inside the hall.

Carlos was down and bleeding. One of the guards was unconscious on the floor, while the other two held bayonets at Carlos, both of them looking like Carlos had given them his money's worth.

Taking control, I tightened the hammerlock on the captain which made him call out in pain. The others turned to look our way.

"Commandeth thy men to stand ho 'r I shall breaketh thy neck." I spoke loudly and firmly into his ear.

"Standeth down guards and dropeth thy weapons." He commanded them.

They reluctantly did as he ordered.

Carlos groaned as he rose from the floor.

"Carlos, how bad are you hurt?" I asked him.

He exposed where he'd placed a hand on his left side. There was blood, but not a great deal.

"I don't think it's deep Joe." He said as he kicked the still unconscious guard. "I'll survive even if this one won't."

"Carlos no time for revenge now. I've got an idea of how we can get back home. Pick up a musket and back me up while we get these locked up."

"No, it's a sword for me. Those damn muskets don't work when you pull the trigger."

It dawned on me what had happened and I half smiled, he'd not cocked the hammer of the musket before he tried to fire it!

"Forget that now. I'll give you some lessons one day."

Speaking to the two freestanding guards, I told them, "Thee two, picketh up thy cousin."

The other two guards did as I commanded them, picking the still incapacitated guard by lifting him up from his underarms.

"All of thee, into the L'rd Keepeth'r's cubiculo."

The two guards moved into the Lord Keepers room, dragging the unconscious one with them.

I followed in with the captain.

"Dropeth thy cousin and then forswear on the flo'r visage down."

They obeyed my command to drop to the floor, lying face down.

I used my free hand to retrieve the gun from my belt again and stuck the nozzle firmly into the captain's neck. "One false moveth from thee mine own captain and thee kicketh the bucket."

I shoved him forward towards the others and immediately fired the gun into the ceiling as a warning shot.

"Down with the oth'rs." I ordered. He dropped to the floor, lying face down next to his men.

I turned to Carlos.

"Is there a key in the door lock?" I asked him

After looking he shook his head. "Nothing there Joe."

Looking at the lock, I thought about how to secure the door to prevent the guards getting out.

Handing the gun to Carlos to watch over the guards, I looked on the outside of the door.

There were plenty of potential hooks in the carvings on the door itself and on the door surrounds.

Back in the Lord Keepers room, I spotted some rope curtain ties and retrieved them off the curtains.

"Come on, Carlos. Let's leave our new found friends to get some rest."

We backed out of the room, closing the door and using the rope from the curtains, I managed to tie the door closed from the outside.

"Hopefully that will keep them long enough. Come on Carlos, I don't feel very welcome here. Think I'll write a letter of complaint to King Charles when we get back to 2025!"

"If we get back." Carlos said solemnly as if he didn't think we would.

"Don't stress so much." I told him, "If we have to stay, well at least you're dressed for the occasion!" It failed to lift his spirits, all he did was groan.

Returning to the banquet hall, I rushed over to where the time travel units stood as I had left them.

I removed the one Carlos had knocked over from the immediate area while I positioned the remaining three units, hoping they would work to form a triangular field of travel without the need of the broken unit. I thought about what the scenario would be if it had been the main unit that Carlos had fallen onto! I had some design changes to seriously think about, if we got back.

Checking over the final positions and ensuring there was enough clearance for the two of us and the fourth unit, I called to Carlos who had been keeping watch as best he could in such a large room.

"If this works Carlos, we'll return to my parent's home where there's some things I need to talk to you about."

"That's fine Joe." He placed a friendly hand on my shoulder. "Anywhere and when but here!"

He moved into the travel area, then stepped away again to retrieve one of the swords, still lying on the banquet room floor.

"Souvenir." He said with a smile and came back into his position.

Shaking my head, but also smiling, I pressed the go button and said out loud, "Good bye 1698 and good riddance!"

We materialized back at mum and dad's place, 2025.

Chapter 24.

"Let's have a look at that bayonet wound first." I told Carlos.

He lifted his 1698 tunic as I went to fetch some hot water, Dettol and other wound cleaning and dressing gear.

"Doesn't look too bad from a layman's point of view. But better get it checked at the hospital though later on."

" Can't do Joe, just clean me up and dress it. No hospital for me. Besides they'll only ask where I got a stab wound and get the cops involved."

"Well maybe you'll change your mind once I've said what I've got to say." I finished cleaning and dressing his wound and put the first aid gear away.

"Come and sit in the lounge Carlos and we can chat."

He sat on the couch as I stood and paced a little in front of him.

"Spit it out Joe."

"I know that you refused to kill Marco and that Infanta was unhappy with you for not doing the job." It was a start!

"I suppose he's still mad at me hey Joe? He said Marco is an undercover cop because he had Sebastian follow him one day and Sebastian took pictures of Marco going and seeing some senior Interpol cop." And besides," He stopped while trying to gather his thoughts as to how to say what he wanted to.

"Besides, I not that kind of a guy, you know Joe. I hear that you have some experience in sports fighting, well I try to keep my – aggressione to inside the ring. I'm no killer Joe, a bad boy as my mama used to say, maybe, but not to kill anyone."

"Glad to hear it Carlos. In fact it's just what I wanted to hear." I thought some more as what next to tell him.

"Marco *is* now dead Carlos, Luigi did the job back in Infanta's study at the mansion. Mrs. Badgley also overheard Infanta and Luigi talk about killing me and leaving you back in 1698 to save them killing you also." I waited for his reaction.

He looked puzzled, then after a moments silence asked, "You think it best for Carlos not to go back to the Infanta dimora (mansion), hey Joe?"

"I very much think it's best for you not to go back Carlos. Actually Carlos I've been thinking that maybe you could help me."

"Hey Joe. You my friend, I've not been back in time with anyone but you." He laughed loudly, I joined him.

"We do have that in common Carlos don't we."

Over the next hour or so, I spilled everything to Carlos. All the fine details, about Mrs. Badgley's exit from the mansion, about how I'd returned originally from 1698 and everyone's reaction, not caring that Carlos was left behind. I told him about my escape from the wine cellar and what I saw and overheard in the hallway and then of my own exit from the mansion. Lastly I told him of the trip to Italy and Interpol and NCA's involvement in the entrapment of Infanta at Heathrow and his confessions.

I let it all sink in while I made us both a coffee.

Taking the mug from me he thanked me and said, "You know Joe. I should have listen to mama. She say, Carlos she say, "'That Infanta man is trouble. He will lead you to bad ways.'" This what she tell me Joe. Carlos -stupid, I didn't listen."

"Not stupid Carlos, maybe a little too easily influenced, but not stupid."

I drank some of my coffee, as did Carlos.

"So what now, Carlos? Do you want to join forces with me in fighting to get Infanta and his gang put away?"

"But I was part of that gang, Joe. Surely the police will put me away also!"

"What if I told you that we could get you a deal?"

"A deal so I wouldn't be put inside you mean?"

"Yes exactly that. Finish your coffee and I'll go and get some of my clothes that I keep here at my parents place for when I'm here, they should fit you, at least casually. And I think they'll be better than what you're currently wearing."

Carlos looked down at his 1698 costume. "Don't know what you saying Joe. Looks perfectly good to me." We both laughed and I went to get him some of my clothes.

As soon as Carlos had changed, we travelled to the maximum time that *I* could travel forward to -

my 'limit date' as I called it, back to where and when Simon was waiting for us.

I realized that if the time travel units were taken into the future by someone else, say Simon or Ms. Walsh, then perhaps at least in theory, I could also go to the future beyond my limit date!

Carlos was safely transported to past his previously thought limit date because the time travel units had already been that far.

Making a mental note to work on this again when Operation Count Your Chickens was over, I told Carlos about introducing him to NCA Senior Sergeant Simon Baxter. He was a little nervous about it, but agreed to speak to Simon.

Calling Simon from upstairs surprised Carlos, he wasn't expecting to meet him so soon. Carlos grabbed for the sword he had brought back from 1698, but I managed to placate him by the time Simon appeared at the bottom of the stairs. "Better I keep that safe for you Carlos for the time being." I told him taking away the sword.

Simon told Carlos that if he turned Crown Witness and hadn't himself committed first or second degree violence crimes, that he would be given immunity from prosecution.

Feeling that Simon already knew that Carlos had only committed misdemeanors, I began to feel that I would never understand why my future self had forbade revealing their knowledge of future case files, it would have made things simpler and quicker.

Still, I bowed to Simon's greater experience with time travel and continued patiently learning.

I had to convince Carlos that a contract wasn't needed and that Simon would keep his word, but Simon told us that he had taken a recording of Carlos' statement and their discussion which would help Carlos if anything happened to Simon himself.

"Have you watched the video of Infanta's entrapment yet?" Simon asked Carlos

"No, it's not necessary. I fully trust Dr. Joe." Carlos replied.

"You should still watch it. It's important to get things exactly right."

"You mean it's in the report?" I asked Simon.

He nodded. "Yes Joe, we have to follow it meticulously just in case!"

As Carlos watched, I wasn't sure if he fidgeted with the joy of seeing Infanta testify against himself or whether it was out of fear, but he twitched and squirmed all though the video.

"Is a good thing we do Joe." Carlos told me after the video recording had finished. "Lorenzo Infanta is a very bad man. He deserves all that's coming to him."

After cooking and eating some food, the three of us chatted for a while. Carlos was very interested in wanting to know more about time travel, the do's and don'ts, the dangers and other 'fun facts'.

We didn't tell him that Simon was from the future, but Simon did divulge a couple of stories, that tickled Carlos, about when he'd gone back to his senior school days in order to sneak some assessment results to his younger self so that he could gain the grades needed to join the police.

I had frowned at the message he was giving to Carlos, time travel wasn't to be used for self-gain, but Simon told me it was what had to occur. He had distinctly remembered receiving a crib sheet before the assessment and no one could work out who had left it for him and on the night after the assessment, the school had been broken into and several assessment submissions, including his - had disappeared, only to re-appear the next day exactly where they had gone missing from.

While confusion had reigned for while at the school, it was all hushed up to prevent a negative report being given about the school's integrity and security and so that the school didn't miss out on the next round of funding!

"Does Director Bedford know about these little trips back in time that you made to further your career?" I asked Simon.

He just changed the subject!

Also during that hour, I had time to text Sam and it wasn't until I did that I realized that she was due into London tomorrow, I looked at the time on my phone. Better make that later today!

By two in the morning, Carlos had fallen asleep on the couch, Simon and I had done a check of the grounds and Applegate and Brown had woken and had eaten the meals that I had cooked them. Simon woke Carlos to introduce him to the two junior constables and then moved him upstairs to rest.

Simon and I then decided to also retire for a rest and stood down from our watch duty in exchange for Applegate and Brown.

I don't know about Simon, but I slept like a log!

Chapter 25.

It was Thursday morning. A summer mist shrouded the New Forest. The birds sang songs of joy and told each other where the best feed was. The ponies munched on the damp vegetation, every so often braying or snorting their welcome to the world. It was going to be a beautiful day!

Okay I'm sorry, a friend asked me not to put any of that type of fluffy stuff in the book, but I just couldn't help myself. The New Forest early on a summer's morning, or indeed on many other mornings, is such a beautiful and idyllic place to be.

But like with most good stories, such a start to a day couldn't last, and this one didn't either.

Assistant Director Walsh had sent a text to Simon that we all should report to the CCP warehouse in Hertfordshire. That included she said, Carlos, myself and all the assigned NCA people.

After loading the time travel equipment into the boot, everyone got into the Pajero and we headed off to Southampton Airport, where Simon was going to meet up with Don and Marie, while Applegate and Brown were to stick with Carlos and me to continue driving up.

We offloaded Simon at 'control post 11' to await the other two and their pilot. I didn't stick around, but headed straight for the M3. Well I did bet Simon that we'd be there before him so it was all go.

Applegate tried to sneak a peek under the blanket I'd used to cover the time travel units.

"Just some experimental equipment for my students to look into." I called out, not wanting them to nosey around. He got the message.

Carlos started to tell Paul and Leroy about his recent adventure.

"Carlos this maybe not the right time to talk about some of the mischievous escapades you've been involved in." I gave him a scolding look. "Really Carlos, you should leave that to talk to Assistant Director Walsh about. She is the one who will be pleading your case with the Crown Prosecution people and she may not want everyone to know about some of the things you've been up to." I winked at him so he'd get my drift about not speaking about the time travelling and play along.

"Of course. Thanks Joe. Sorry gentlemen, but the boss has said I need to keep quiet for my own good!"

Both Applegate and Brown hadn't any other idea about what we were talking about, so accepted that they were going to be left out of the loop this time.

A couple of miles before the Poyle turnoff on the M25, the traffic slowed down considerably.

Slowly, all vehicles were re-directed off the motorway and onto the Stanwell Moor Road which runs at the back of Heathrow and up to the M4 access via the Colnbrook bypass.

Turning on the radio for the road reports, revealed that a huge semi-trailer had jack knifed, then overturned onto its side and completely blocked the M25 northbound causing long delays and detours.

Now that really frustrated me, Simon was going to win the bet!

Then things really went crazy.

As I drove onto the Langley Roundabout to double-back towards the west bound lanes on the M4 to eventually get back on the M25 further up, we were hit hard by a utility truck!

Blacking out for a few seconds, my airbag inflated saving my bacon, however Paul Applegate who was sitting directly behind me got the full force of the impact.

I sat still for a while, the shock just forcing my body and mind into stillness.

I heard screams and sirens. I heard voices, people asking questions, someone taking charge, metal and glass screeching and breaking. A helicopter possibly directly overhead or was some cutting tool, it was all a blur, but I do clearly remember one word that Carlos said before he passed out. "Moretti"

After being lifted out of the car, I was taken on a gurney to outside an ambulance parked close by.

"Dr. Bedford, can you hear me?" the paramedic asked shining a light into my eyes.

"What the hell happened?" I replied, knowing the answer to my question as soon as I'd asked it.

"Don't concern yourself with that now. Do you feel any pain anywhere?"

I mean what a stupid question. My car had just been rammed by a ute, probably doing about fifty miles per hour. Of course I'm hurting!

Trying to rise from the gurney, a firm hand helped me back down.

"Just lie still for a moment while we get a neck brace on you. We need to get you to hospital for some x-rays." Then to another paramedic he said, "Take that one over to the chief, he'll want to have a look before he's taken to the morgue."

"Who died, tell me?" I tried getting up again but this met with the same response as before.

"Please you may have damaged your spine, stay still for me until we can secure you."

I saw another paramedic pass my man a neck brace from inside the ambulance, which he fitted to my neck.

"Just the straps to go and then you're on your way for those x-rays and anything else that's needed. Looks from the outside that apart from a load of cuts on your face and hands, that you are a very lucky man." He leant over me and smiled. "But we won't count our chickens just yet will we?" He said.

I laughed at a sudden realization. Operation Count your Chickens was Director Bedford's name for the mass arrests operation. I had chosen it!

The gurney was rolled into the ambulance and the paramedic waiting inside started doing her checks on my blood pressure and everything.

I heard the ambulance door close behind me and the paramedic introduced herself as Sarah then called to the driver up front. "All good Clive let's go."

As I lay back in the ambulance I became aware of the emergency strobe lights flashing on the outside. The engine started up, the siren activated and off we went.

As the paramedic reached for my I.D., I called out "Sarah," to get her attention.

"Yes Joe what is it?" she queried possibly thinking that I was needing medical attention.

"The three others in my car, are they alright? I need to know."

"I think they've been taken out of the vehicle and are being assessed. They'll soon be on their way to Hillingdon Hospital's A&E department, which is where we're taking you. Other than that, I'm sorry I don't know." She put my I.D. back into my jacket pocket.

Letting it rest, I started a self-examination as best I could being restricted in the gurney straps.

Nothing seemed to be broken. I did have some pain starting in various areas of my face and right hand, probably the cuts I thought. Everything else seemed okay.

Then I remembered it was Thursday and my darling fiancé was flying into Gatwick today.

"What time is it, Sarah?" I asked.

Sarah looked at her wristwatch, "9.15, you will go and do these things at peak traffic hours won't you Mr. Joe Public." She smiled.

"It's Dr. Joe Public if you don't mind." Replying also with a smile.

"Sorry 'doctor' Joe. Where is your practice, anywhere near here?"

"I'm a doctor of physics, not medicine. But yes I suppose I'm still practicing in my field. It's at the Cavendish Laboratory, West Cambridge where I'm a Reader."

She bent forward towards me, "Well it's good to know that you're coherent Dr. Bedford."

She looked outside. "Won't be long now, we're almost there. I'm sure they'll get you in pretty quickly for those x-rays. Hope you didn't plan on a party tonight though!"

"Actually the whole day was going to be one big party in one way or another. I guess things will have to be shuffled around a bit."

Sarah tutted, "And just when I was in need of a good social gathering."

"Sorry another time maybe." I then remembered the time travel equipment. "Say Sarah, what will happen to my car?"

"I'm certain the lead investigator for the accident will be in touch with you once the hospital has checked you out. They should give you all that information. It looked from what I saw though is, well I hope you've got replacement cover because that car isn't going anywhere being driven!"

Groaning at the news, Sarah asked if there were any changes in how I felt and began taking my pulse.

"No, nothing's changed except for the bad news keeps getting worse."

"It's early days Joe. Given time and you'll look back at today and see the good bits shining through. Like meeting me for instance."

"Steady on old girl." I joked, putting on an Italian accent. "I'm a soon to be married man. I *was* hoping to pick up my fiancé from Gatwick this evening."

"Shucks, all the good ones get taken. Oh and less of the old girl, I'm only 58, I've got lots of life in me yet. Okay here we are, soon be time for us to say our goodbyes. Hope you don't forget me Joe."

"Forget you Sarah, how could I!"

Chapter 26.

The Accident and Emergency was about half full when I was wheeled in, from what I could detect. I was seen straight away by the Triage nurse and taken straight for x-rays to see if my neck or spine were damaged. After which they wheeled me back into A & E to await the results.

And wait and wait. It seemed like forever. All the time I listened out for the sound of a voice of one of the other three in the car with me. Nothing! Only the general sounds of a busy hospital ED. A child crying while also being comforted by an adult, what sounded like a young person probably drugged up to the hilt and arguing with the medical staff that they didn't want their help, they were using much more colourful language than that, but you've more than likely heard the sort of thing yourself.

A male voice called for a saline drip, another male voice told someone they had to wait because there had been two serious road accidents that were given more priority than their 'little cut'.

A woman's voice called for someone to be 'taken upstairs'. There were banging sounds, someone dropped a metal utensil which clanged onto the floor and then they apologized profusely to the doctor.

That's what I was hearing, but all I could see was the ceiling with its bright lights, air conditioning vent, a security camera and sprinkler system.

A nurse came to check my vitals.

"Any results from the x-rays yet nurse?" I enquired.

"Not yet Dr. Bedford, they shouldn't be long." The nurse didn't stick around for further conversation.

The curtain surrounding me started moving on my left side as someone walked around the cubicle next to mine.

"Mr. Antonio, are you with us Mr. Antonio?"

"No 'I'm with the Woolwich'! Where do you think I am?"

"Smarty, I've not heard that saying since my grandma died years ago. Where did you pick it up from?"

"The old lady cook back in the house I live in, Mrs. Badgley. She says it all the time!"

The voice with its Italian accent was unmistakable.

"Carlos is that you?" I called out.

"Hey Joe, you next door to me! How you doing Joe, you cut up badly, any broken bones?"

"Too early to say Carlos. I'm waiting x-ray results. What about yourself?"

"Ah Joe. They give Carlos an old grumpy nurse. What happened to all the pretty ones?"

"Sounds like you're just fine Carlos. Try and behave yourself my friend. Say Carlos, did you notice what happened to the equipment at the back of the car?"

"Sorry Joe. I was out for a few minutes and didn't come round until they'd put me in an ambulance. Don't worry everything is safe if not sound Joe."

I rolled my eyes right at another familiar voice. "Hey Carlos, look who's here. It's your favourite policeman Senior Sergeant Baxter. Hello Simon, suppose you came to brag about winning our little bet."

"No, not really. No one has reached the CCP HQ yet, so no one's won yet. I came straight from the airstrip to here." Simon replied.

A doctor came into view holding some papers. "Doctor Bedford, I'm Dr. Kate Milligan, we've just got your x-rays back, but I need to take a closer look at them." Then she turned to Simon, winked her eyes at him and said, "NCA, not the usual road accident investigation department."

"I'm not investigating the crash. These three are NCA team members." Simon informed her.

"These three? You mean these four don't you Simon?"

Dr. Milligan left to check the x-ray report.

"Joe, Paul Applegate was killed in the accident. Leroy's unconscious still, at the other end of the A & E ward. Sorry, but with Carlos here, it's only three."

We were silent for a few moments. Walsh's words 'we won't be happy with all of the outcomes', came to mind.

"He died instantly on impact Joe. He wouldn't have known a thing about it. Coralie has gone herself to tell his parents and siblings."

Some heavy footsteps approached. "Gentlemen, I'm Sergeant Alan Smalley - road policing lead investigator. We don't see too much of

NCA these days around here," he said to Simon. He didn't wink his eyes!

Simon shook his hand. "Senior Sergeant Simon Baxter, this is Dr. Joe Bedford, and next door is Carlos Antonio, both NCA team members. Detective Constable Leroy Brown is down the other end of the ED ward, also on the NCA payroll. Sergeant Smalley, what happened out there? Any ideas as yet?"

"It's a bit early to say, but you were hit by a ute Dr. Bedford, driven by someone known to us as a heavy meth user. He died on impact like your other colleague. Until we do more tests, we won't be able to say for sure, but it just looks like you were in the wrong place at the wrong time."

"Alan, do you know what happened to my vehicle, there was some expensive experimental gear in the back?"

"Yes," He took out a small notepad. "We got a call from an Assistant Director Walsh to get it towed to somewhere up near Rickmansworth. She your boss?"

"She thinks she is." I replied rather flippantly.

"Yes, Assistant Director Walsh is the one we report to." Simon added, shaking his head at me.

"Well I'll go and see what my guys have got from the scene of the accident and I'll get back to you. Senior Sergeant, do you want me to give a copy of the report of my findings to you or to this Assistant Director Walsh?"

Simon gave the accident investigator his card, "No, to me will be fine thank you Sergeant Smalley. That's as long as any other heir apparent to the boss title doesn't object?" He said turning to look at me.

I smiled at Simon's quip.

"Sounds like you NCA folk are as crazy as us road cops." Sergeant Smalley said as he turned away.

We remained silent for a while as the news of Paul's death sank in.

Then looking at Simon I asked, "Was this in that future report Simon? Be honest with me now."

Simon moved a little closer. "Joe, we've both mentioned before, even you as Director Bedford have said many times, not to try and change timeline outcomes."

"We could have prevented his death Simon. It didn't need to be this way."

I'd hardly known Paul, but that didn't matter. He was on my team. I should have protected him better, even though his job was my protection.

Dr. Milligan came over. "I'm going to ask you gentlemen to keep it down. We have some really sick people in here and you guys are making a racket. Please."

She looked firm and in control. Simon looked impressed and interested.

"Simon, your married to your job aren't you?" I said with a grin.

Simon blushed. It was good to see, he was still a man of honour and perhaps a little innocent. Rare qualities these days.

"I'll go next door and speak to Carlos." He said, moving behind the curtain to the left.

I thought I heard him add, "I will sort you out later Joe," under his breath, but it could have been just my imagination!

"Now Dr. Bedford." Dr. Milligan said.

"Yes Dr. Milligan." I replied smiling.

"It seems your x-rays are all clear, so good news there. We will want to keep you in overnight just to make sure, sometimes after accidents like this, injuries don't make themselves manifest to us until hours later plus you are a little concussed still."

"But I have to collect my fiancé from the airport later. I will have to come back another time to stay for breakfast."

"You'll do as Dr. Milligan tells you to do Dr. Bedford, that's my order."

The voice came from out of sight behind Dr. Milligan, who turned around to see who was there. It was Coralie Walsh.

Walsh moved to my bedside and turned to Dr. Milligan.

'Dr. Milligan, I'm Assistant Director Walsh, currently Dr. Bedford's boss, do you think we could have a little privacy please." It wasn't a question.

Dr. Milligan nodded. "I'll come back later." She told me and then disappeared out of view.

"Why Assistant Director Walsh, why? He could have been saved. You knew it was going to happen." I was angry still.

"Yes, I could have told you to be more careful. To watch for a white utility truck coming from your right hand side at the Langley roundabout. You know why I didn't tell you Dr. Bedford, we can't change things like that."

"How do we live with that Walsh, how can we go on travelling back and forth in time, knowing, but not being able to do anything like save our own team members, our own family? Do you understand at all how I'm feeling?"

She took a deep breath then for the first time I saw Coralie Walsh shed tears from her eyes.

"And how do you think I feel? I'm the one who assigned Mr. Applegate to your security detail. I'm the one who personally ordered him to travel with you in your car. How do you think I'll feel in eleven years' time when I have to see my own husband killed because of a decision that I had made, knowing that I could change what was about to happen if I wanted to risk history being re-written."

Silence.

Even the sounds of the ED ward seemed to vanish at that moment.

I felt a like total idiot.

"Coralie." I said with tears in my own eyes now. "I'm so sorry." I swallowed. "I – I didn't think clearly. Please forgive me."

She opened her hand bag and pulled out two clean white handkerchiefs.

Passing one to me, she told me, "You'll give me this one in eleven years when you comfort me over Frank's death. You cried then too. You and Frank are going to.."

I held up one hand to dry my face and the other to stop her saying anymore.

Looking at the handkerchief she'd given me, I saw it had my initials embroidered on it.

"Should I give it you back now or keep it for that time?"

She held out her hand. "Give it back please. I know where you get it from in the future and it's not the here and now."

She had wiped her own eyes dry and was looking more composed.

"*I'm* going to meet up with Samantha and Giorgio at the airport later. You need to be cleaned up still for when I bring her back here. Well, upstairs in the ward anyway." She turned to leave, then turned back again.

"Get the Doctor to check on some of those cuts on your face. You don't want any glass left in, there's no telling what damage they could do." She winked at me.

"Coralie?"

"Yes *Joe*, Dr. Bedford."

"You once said that we are to become good friends in the future."

"That's what I said." She nodded.

"Well I feel we've made both a shaky and a solid start to that friendship here and now."

"Don't push it, I'm still your boss for another few months yet." She reached out and gave my hand a squeeze, smiled and left.

Chapter 27.

Simon returned to my cubicle. He looked like the cat that got the cream.

"Kate told me both you and Carlos are going to be fine, if a little bruised." He told me.

"Kate. First name terms is it?"

He smiled. "There's a natural bond between us Joe. You can't just let that sort of thing pass you by."

"Simon, do I have to remind you that you don't belong in this particular time. When you get back to your time, 'Kate' will be in her mid-fifties and probably married with seven kids."

"Just having a bit of fun Joe, that's all. You can't blame me for trying."

"Well try in your own time period. It'll be better for all concerned."

Simon changed the subject.

"Carlos is being wheeled up to the first floor ward. You're going to be joining him soon. I'll go and get a coffee. I'll see you up there." He sounded a little sheepish, chastised maybe!

"Tell Kate, *Dr. Milligan* to please come and see me."

"You're not going to tell her…"

"Don't stress Simon, I need some medical attention. I'm fine really just something a little bird told me that needs looking at, and I won't mention anything to her about anything to do with you." I interrupted him, and then added, "I have no rights to meddle in your personal affairs Simon. I'm sorry, it's probably just the day we're all having."

He nodded smiling, "See you in fifteen or so."

Dr. Milligan came over a few minutes later. "I believe your highness rang." She said with a smile.

I ignored the bait. "I'm feeling some irritations on my face. You couldn't look at what's going on can you?"

"I'll get Nurse Singh to come and have a look." She departed again.

Another couple of minutes wait and a male nurse walked over to my bedside carrying a tray of something.

"Good morning Dr. Bedford." he said very cheerfully. "My name is Singh, Nurse Rohan Singh at your very service Dr. Bedford. Dr. Milligan asked me to take a closer look at some of your facial lacerations from the accident. She tells me you have irritations, no?"

"Irritations, yes," I replied. "They're difficult to pinpoint, maybe take a look at each cut and see if you find anything, please Rohan."

He put the tray down and picked up one of those magnifying glass headbands with a light attached to it and put it on.

"Just lay still please Dr. Bedford, I'll see what I can find."

He leant over me with the light shining on my face.

"Oh yes, keep still please, I can see a small piece of glass there in this little cut." He reached out without looking and picked up small tweezer and went to work on my face.

"Got him," Rohan called out in glee. "Just checking that this one is all clear now."

He went through the process of investigating each cut from the accident, finding and removing five glass splinters.

"You're lucky I'm on duty today Dr. Bedford, I'm the best splinter removing nurse in all the NHS. That's official!" He claimed proudly giving his head a wobble Indian style and with the biggest grin.

"Then I'm very lucky, thank you Rohan." I smiled back, genuinely grateful.

"I'll just clean your face up a little Dr. Bedford. I don't think any of the cuts need to be dressed, we'll see." He said.

Nurse Singh finished his task of cleaning up my face, only one cut required dressing. He then unstrapped me from the hospital bed and removed the neck brace. "Thanks." I told him rubbing the stiffness from my neck and shoulders.

It felt really good to be moving again although I stayed lying down for the moment. Nurse Singh picked up all the equipment he'd brought in and then he turned to depart.

"Thank you again Rohan, I'll mention you in dispatches." He giggled at that and gave me another head wobble as he disappeared from sight.

I slowly rose up from the lying position to sit on the edge of the bed.

The immediate reaction I felt was dizziness and the desire to vomit. I lay down again.

Dr. Milligan came over to the cubicle. "That'll teach you. You probably want one of these now." She offered me a white plastic sick bag with a solid ring opening.

"No thanks." I told her, then changed my mind, "Oh maybe just leave it with me, just in case." I reached out for it and tucked it under the pillow.

"Feeling a little dizziness, I suspect. It's normal for someone whose head has been assaulted by a truck plowing into them at speed. We get a lot of it from sports people, rugby in particular, who are concussed after a heavy tackle."

"Remind me never to take up rugby."

"It'll pass in a while, just stay lying down until we suggest otherwise."

"How is Leroy Brown doing?" I asked her.

"Better. He's awake now, but we're going to have to re-set his left arm and a couple of stitches for a head cut. He'll probably be concussed longer than yourself. All in all the three of you came out of this pretty lightly, normally there's much more serious injuries and more than one death."

"One death is one too many."

"I didn't mean it to sound disrespectful of your colleague." She became sheepish, lowering her head.

"No, I know you didn't, don't stress on it. I appreciate your comments. Yes we are very fortunate not to be in a much worse condition than we are."

I had to agree with Simon, she seemed like a good match for him, only the time period difference was definitely not right!

Eventually, I was moved upstairs next to Carlos in a ward of four beds, we being the only occupants at present.

The hospital was in a bit of a dilapidated condition, a new hospital was in the process of being built, but with the covid-19 issues restricting the progress – well that was the politicians and contractors excuse anyway, it had been delayed and not expected to be finished until early 2027.

The ward we were in was part of a temporary refurbishment to tide things over, so was one of the better wards to be in, special treatment for NCA? It did make me wonder though. Should I have gone into politics instead? The people making these decisions to spend big with public funds! How many times has someone said, 'I could do a better job'! But then again as my dad used to say when I was a boy, "Put up or shut up. If you think you can do better, do it!"

Carlos and I chatted for a while. He was touched by Simon telling Dr. Milligan that he was with the NCA. "Did Simon mean what he said Joe?"

"About you being part of the team, of course he did. The more you get to know about Simon Baxter's uncanny ways, the more you'll come to like and respect him." I nearly told him about Simon being a time traveler, but stopped short. Maybe later.

Eventually we both dozed off to sleep, the stress of the day catching up.

When I awoke Simon was sitting in a visitors chair next to my bed reading something on his phone.

I glanced over to Carlos who was still away with the fairies.

"Doing research on Dr. Kate?" I asked Simon who hadn't noticed that I had woken.

"Wouldn't you like to give me an earful if I was! Hi Joe, how are things going?" He replied smiling. "It's a text from Coralie, firstly it's been decided that Operation Count Your Chickens will go ahead tomorrow morning, 0700 prompt."

"She's not one to hang about is she! And second?"

"Second is that she's at the airport, your Samantha and her brother Giorgio have landed and probably going through customs right now. She'll bring them directly here when they're cleared through."

"Any third?"

"Yes, it's a bit strange though. She said to tell you it's okay to mention to Carlos that I'm from the future, and not to hold anything back from him."

Talk about Simon's uncanniness! It was then it dawned on me, my future self was in consultation with Walsh all along. I was leading this whole performance, following the report script from A to Z.

Again I seriously thought at that very moment of going straight to my lab, making adjustments to my prototype time travel units and going back to convince my younger self to stick with martial arts and forget physics all together!

I didn't. Instead I composed myself and started readying my attention on when Sam walked into the ward.

My future self obviously never went back to stop this mad, crazy chain of events. Something, sometime in the future was going to convince me it was worth keeping going on with this time travel game!

And then I instantly knew that that something was having Samantha in my life. I also knew it was the right thing to do. The world would be a much better place without Lorenzo Infanta on the loose. Yes, I wasn't happy with some of the outcomes like Paul's death. But how many future victims will be relieved of their suffering because Infanta was going to be locked up, which without the time travel work, would not happen!

Chapter 28.

That afternoon when Sam rushed into the ward, my feelings were confirmed. Without developing the time travel units, I wouldn't have the most wonderful girl ever as my soon to be wife.

She of course was extremely upset about the accident, but after finding out that I was going to be fine, calmed herself down.

Now sitting up in the hospital bed without any dizziness, I told Sam of all my earlier misgivings concerning time travel and how I had felt that this had led to Paul's death and that I had wanted to go back and stop all of this, but that risked not only losing her, but it was also a big timeline changer. The price was too high, especially losing her, she hugged me for that.

Now further developing time travel and using it to help with crime prevention was my new committed work focus, putting lecturing at Cavendish down the list of priorities.

I mentioned also that I needed to have the Cavendish connection until Coralie Walsh, nee Ashton was well and truly on board.

After listening to my reveal, Sam fully confirmed her support for my decision to continue on as future director of the CCP team, as long as she was somewhere in the picture also. When she asked about joining us on the team, I joked about Gibb's rule number twelve, 'Not dating a co-worker', to which she rightly corrected me, that if we were married, we technically wouldn't be dating. You girls always have an answer don't you!

While Sam and I were talking, Coralie Walsh introduced Giorgio to Simon as they chatted with Carlos.

I found out later that Ms. Walsh had formally offered both Carlos and Giorgio roles in the new department, everyone it seems wanted in. Carlos was offered a role as part of Simon's security team and Giorgio as a safe house coordinator and minder for people in protective care.

Thinking at first that Giorgio's new role was a little superfluous, maybe 'one for the boys', I quickly realized that Walsh would know the future and that the role was probably going to suit Giorgio down to the ground or have some very specific future purpose.

And Carlos, well he was so delighted he hugged his new boss – for the first and last time going by the look on Walsh's face. I got the distinct impression that Carlos had never before been given such a vote of confidence, there was definitely tears in his eyes!

Finally all six of us got together as Ms. Walsh told us about Operation Count Your Chickens – she confirmed my suspicions that it was I that had named it! I couldn't blame anyone else. I'll never live that one down, although it seemed much more appropriate after the paramedic who first attended me had spoken the phrase.

With everyone in place, starting at 0700 the next morning - UK time, Lorenzo Infanta, any suspected infiltrators and all of the crime gang would be arrested and charged.

Walsh and Simon then said their goodbyes, leaving Giorgio in charge of taking care of Sam and I until Carlos was discharged from the hospital. They both then went off to make final preparations for tomorrow.

Sometime later in the evening Leroy was moved into a third bed in the room. He was in and out of consciousness and with a blue dressing covering his head cuts and an arm in plaster.

The next morning Carlos and I were discharged.

Sam had stayed overnight at the hospital, while Giorgio had spent overnight in a local Airbnb after hiring a car for us all to use.

Giorgio arrived at the hospital at about 8.30 a.m. with a bag of Danish pastries and some half decent coffee for each of us. Carlos enjoyed the bulk of the goodies!

We stuck around for a while awaiting news concerning Operation Count Your Chickens, but nothing was forthcoming, so we kept Leroy company for a while until both his girlfriend and his mother arrived.

By the time we left the hospital it was 10.30 and still no news concerning the arrests.

I decided to take the lead and suggested that the four of us should go and get some clean clothes, which for me was back at my place near Reigate.

Sam and Giorgio had their own luggage from the airport, but all of Carlos' belongings were at the Infanta mansion with his wallet.

Rather than going back and risk running into Infanta, I treated him to new clothes which looked much better than my old sloppy joes he'd been wearing since I'd given them to him in exchange for his 1698 costume in Lyndhurst.

So the four of had some fresh clothes on but with still no news from Walsh or Simon, this was starting to get a little frustrating.

I thought about calling them, but we all agreed it was probably best to wait their call, especially if things were getting messy with the arrests.

We just had to be patient.

"Okay, let's go to Cavendish. I'm feeling a bit naked without the time travel units. I've got a couple of prototypes there that could be used at a pinch after a few adjustments. Then we can head for the warehouse and check the main time units and my car out and of course hopefully Walsh and Simon are back by then."

No-one objected to my suggestions so off we went.

Giorgio was driving with Carlos up front while Sam and I got comfortable on the back seat. No comments out there please!

We got as far as Egham on the M25 when Giorgio finally received the call.

He asked Carlos to answer the phone while he pulled over so he could hear above the traffic noise.

Simon was asking for assistance. He was with Brunelli and they had cornered Danny and other gang members and needed someone to distract them, it seemed all other law enforcement people were tied up elsewhere.

It sounded urgent, but it also sounded a bit risky even suspicious. I mean what could we do, we had no training, no weapons and I'd even taken off the protective gear so all of us were vulnerable to being shot.

"I'm not willing to risk Sam." I told the others firmly.

Carlos pointed to another car hire place only about a hundred metres away, "Maybe we can split up, Giorgio go with Sam and hire another car and Joe and I go and help Simon."

"We've already got both our names down for this hire car." Giorgio said, "We probably won't be able to hire another until this one is returned."

"I don't have any I.D. on me, unless you can count letters from the king in 1689!" Carlos still had the letters with him from the trip back then.

Sam hadn't bothered getting her license yet since she'd been chauffeured everywhere.

"Well I'll go with Sam and continue onto the lab, while you two take this car to help Simon."

"But Joe," Giorgio started to object.

"No Giorgio,' I countered starting to get out of the car. "We don't have time. Simon needs the help. Come on Sam, I've got plenty enough I.D. Carlos google the address where Simon is, you're the navigator now!"

I helped Sam out of the car, with both Giorgio and Carlos' objections falling on deaf ears.

"Go." I called out slapping the side of the car.

They drove off as Sam and I started to walk towards the car hire company.

All that was available for hire was a ute and a transit van. Seems I was destined to drive one of these Fords vans after all, especially since white utes were currently off my favourites list.

We headed off towards the lab, despite my gut feeling things were not quite what they should be.

Chapter 29.

Another thing that Gibbs used to say is, 'listen to your gut'.

Well hindsight they say is a wonderful thing!

The university was into its third week of the summer break, there was only a skeleton crew of staff on board, but when I saw that there was no one at the security desk – why on earth didn't I take Samantha by the hand and turn and run!

We didn't. We walked straight up to my lab on the first floor with the coffee and snacks we purchased at the vending machines.

Gathering together the prototypes I'd built of the time travel equipment, I hooked one up to my computer to make some necessary adjustments.

Sam looked on patiently trying to understand as I gave commentary on what I was doing and why.

A clanging noise drew our attention. "Hello Martin is that you?" I called out thinking it was Martin Jenkins. There was no reply.

"It could be the cleaner." Sam suggested.

"It might be best if I investigate. You go into the office and lock the door behind you." I told her.

"You think it could be one of Uncle Lorenzo's men?"

"It could be. I'd rather not wait to find out when they came to us. If there is one of Lorenzo's men out there, I want to meet him on my terms."

"Be careful. We could even call the police." Sam started to worry.

"I think by the time they got here, whatever is going to happen will have happened." I gave her a kiss on the forehead. "Into the office with you and take the time travel unit with you. It's almost finished."

I stealthily made my way to the corridor and looked either way. The sound, I thought had come from towards the lift well to the right.

There was no-one in sight but I crept forward, turning to look back every so often in case I'd been wrong about the direction.

Stopping to unhook a fire extinguisher from the wall, I passed Martin's office – it was empty.

Past his laboratory, also empty – I edged closer to the lift well, feeling my heart pumping strongly and wishing it would keep down the noise!

Arriving at the junction of corridors where the lift well was located, I peered around the corner, keeping my back close to the wall.

A cleaner lay on the floor, blood trickling slowly from his head making a small pool on the tiles.

The cleaners mop was on the floor and his bucket overturned about a couple of meters away with its contents spilled all over.

What's that?

The lights reflected some foot marks leading into the male washroom.

With one eye on the washroom door I knelt to check the cleaner's condition. He was unconscious but alive with a fairly strong pulse.

Moving towards the toilet door, I pointed the nozzle of the fire extinguisher towards the men's washroom and used my foot to open the door gently.

As the door opened more, I caught sight of someone behind the door in the washroom mirror and pushed the door hard onto the person behind, knocking them over as two shots rang out - one shattering the mirror, the other hitting I don't know where.

Turning quickly to face the assailant, I pulled the trigger of the fire extinguisher, spraying him with foam.

Another shot hit me in the arm forcing me to drop the fire extinguisher and fall to my knees clutching my arm.

Seeing the shooter's face covered with foam gave me energy, so standing I kicked the gun from his hand while he couldn't see.

Another kick into his midriff made him cry out and double over on the floor.

With my good arm, I wrestled him over onto his stomach and held his hands behind his back with my knee then grabbing hold of his foam soaked hair, I banged his head hard down onto the tiles.

He lay still, unconscious underneath me.

Reaching for his lost gun with my injured arm, the pain was excruciating. I changed to my right hand and picked the gun up, wiping it dry on my shirt.

The man on the floor stirred so I used his gun butt to give him a better sleep!

Satisfied that he was out for a good while, I put the gun into my jacket pocket and turned the guy over.

Wanting to see his face, I grabbed some paper towels and wiped the foam from his face. "Gian-Luca! I thought you were locked up safely already."

It was Infanta's doorman. Had he been bailed or escaped, I didn't know.

Pulling off his belt, I managed with my one good arm to secure his hands behind his back.

The floor was a mess with my blood now mixing with the foam.

Standing, I cautiously exited the men's washroom to go to the first aid station located on the other side of the lift well, past the ladies washroom.

Taking a few items, I stuffed them into my jacket pocket after taking the gun out and resting it on top of the first aid cupboard.

Suddenly a scream, It was Sam.

Snatching the gun back up, I ran back towards my lab.

As I entered the lab, I saw Lorenzo Infanta with arm around Sam and holding a gun to her head.

"You bastard." I called out, "Hurt Sam and I'll make you suffer."

"My, we are in a temper aren't we? I thought Joseph, that you would be dead by now. I hope you haven't hurt Gian-Luca, he has a court appearance on Monday to attend."

Sam cursed and struggled unsuccessfully to free herself.

"Now, now Samantha darling, don't be like that. Uncle Lorenzo doesn't want to make this any harder than he has to."

"Give me that gun and I'll make sure I make it much easier for you." She argued bravely. "Joe you're hurt. Let go you monster, Joe needs help."

"Ah the happy couple, wanting to be with each other. So nice to see family happy together."

"We're not your family. Sam's right – you're nothing but a monster, even killing your own brother and sister-in-law."

The shocking news I blurted out gave Sam some new impetus.

She lifted a foot of the ground and planted a stiletto heal into Infanta's foot.

As he yelled, she swiped at the gun and then elbowed him in the gut. "You - killed my parents?" She then said something in Italian, the first and only time I heard her swear!

I joined in bringing my right arm to bear down on his back.

As he fell forward, he shot the gun, the wild round catching me in the right leg.

"Joe." Sam screamed.

"I'm good," I answered, not very convincingly.

Another shot, this time hitting Sam in her side. She screamed and went down on one knee.

This shot was from behind me. Turning quickly I saw Brunelli moving out of my line of fire as I shot a couple of rounds in his direction.

I pushed Infanta to the ground, collected Sam with my good arm and retreated to the office, slamming the door behind us.

We both sat on the floor behind my desk nursing our wounds.

Sam's side was just grazed fortunately, but I cleaned up the blood with the things I'd picked from the first aid cupboard.

She then attended to my wounds. My leg was also just grazed, but my left arm was more serious. "We'll have to get you to a hospital," she said doing the best she could to dress it with what we had.

We sat on the floor with our backs to the wall and our eyes closed, protected from view by the desk.

Then turning to each other we kissed briefly and took deep breaths.

"Brunelli. He was the infiltrator all the time. Giorgio told me not to trust the Italian police."

"I hadn't realized getting involved with you was going to be so much fun." Sam told me smiling.

I brushed the hair from her eyes, kissed her again and replied, "Wait till you see my party tricks!"

We both sat quietly again for a moment, hurting from our wounds.

"Hey I've been thinking, maybe we should move to Australia, I mean when all this is over."

"You keep thinking Butch, that's what you're good at." Sam answered trying to pull a Robert Redford impersonation off.

We both laughed. If we survived this day, there were good signs for our future together. At least we both shared a similar sense of humour!

"Shall we go and face the music?" she asked.

"As long as we don't end up like Butch and Sundance, I'm good to go."

Sam got up carefully and turned to help me up. We both complained as we rose to a squat position still behind the desk.

We kissed again. "I love you Joe Bedford."

"I love you too Samantha Infanta. Got to get that surname changed though!"

"I'm getting married soon. I'll be Mrs. Bedford then." She said with pride in her voice.

"Mr. Bedford is surely a lucky fellah."

"He'd better believe it."

We smiled again and I poked my head up slowly to see into the lab.

No-one in sight!

Standing I encouraged Sam to stay low while I investigated the others whereabouts.

Infanta came out from behind a tall cupboard with his gun pointing at me.

Not giving him a chance I fired a shot that hit him in the chest and down he went.

As Brunelli appeared crouching low from behind the work bench, I pulled the trigger of Gian-Luca's gun – nothing, it was empty!

Brunelli stood up, pointing the gun directly at me.

"So Dr. Bedford, this is where it all ends for you and your little bride to be." He smiled as he said it, ignoring Infanta's groans as he lay face down on the floor.

Moving over to the lab door, Brunelli opened it and quickly glanced down the corridor in both directions.

"Fortunately we've already taken care of security and the cleaning staff. Come on out Ms. Infanta, you can at least die in each other's arms. We won't get anyone else disturbing us."

Brunelli was enjoying himself now. "You must learn to check how many rounds you have in your gun before you start shooting at someone Joe, I have two more in mine, one for each of you.”

“And you think you’re going to get away with all this, Brunelli? You won’t be able to run forever – the police WILL catch up with you someday.”

“I think that they might have a hard time finding Malcolm Brunelli, Dr. Bedford.” As he spoke, he pulled away from his face a rubber latex mask revealing a totally different person. “You see Dr. Bedford, what’s left of the real Malcolm Brunelli is swimming in a vat of sulphuric acid somewhere in Milan. While little ‘ol me will get clean away, after I’ve taken a few investments from the Infanta house that is.”

Sam had come over to stand by my side. “So who do we have the not-pleasure of speaking with?” she asked.

“Mario Moretti, at your service.” Our new assailant replied. “I think you know my brother Tommaso. We are the new owners of Infanta’s business interests. And I must thank you Dr. Bedford for taking care of that little job for me.” He kicked at Infanta’s now lifeless body.

Moretti started to walk closer towards us. “I’m afraid for you both that, now the time has come to say goodbye." He raised the gun and pointed it straight at me.

"Bye, bye Dr. Bedford."

A gun shot sounded but nothing came from Moretti's gun.

Instead his face immediately turned a pallor that could only mean one thing.

First his gun dropped from his hand onto the floor. Then he himself fell forward, stiff as a board.

Sam and I were glad to see what we saw next.

Standing behind Moretti was Coralie Walsh, gun in hand.

"If everything was to go according to the report," she said. "You two now kiss, while I call for an ambulance to take you both to hospital."

She smiled and turned lifting her phone to her ear as she did.

Sam and I turned to each other and kissed, long and hard.

"That's enough of that." Walsh commanded as she returned from making the call.

She went into the office and retrieved the time travel prototype.

"We need to dispense with this before the boys in blue get here Dr. Bedford. In the lab safe?"

I nodded and handed her the key. "Does the report say anything about where we go for our honeymoon Ms. Walsh?"

"Australia, Dr. Bedford, Australia."

She turned and began walking towards the lift. "Coming?" she called out.

Chapter 30.

Over the next few days we learnt that Operation Count Your Chickens had been a success.

Yes there were several hiccups along the way.

Danny had pretended to be Simon when he'd called Giorgio's phone to 'get help'. The fact that it was Carlos that answered didn't matter, he'd only had brief contact with Simon as well so either of them could have been excused for mistaking Danny for Simon, especially while driving on a busy, noisy road.

It had been Infanta's ploy to separate the four of us to get Sam and me by ourselves.

Some of the gang in Italy had managed to hold out in a warehouse for about six hours before they finally got their comeuppance.

Another individual in France had managed to escape police only to have been seriously injured trying to jump onto a moving train heading for Barcelona.

As well as injuries to Sam and myself, three law enforcers had been also been shot. Two of them seriously injured of which one who later died as a result. Yet despite bullets flying all over Europe, no civilians were hurt, thankfully.

The culmination of it all was that every single one of Infanta's group were either dead or had been arrested.

We also learnt that the drugged up driver of the ute that plowed into us had been on Infanta's payroll, and supervised by Mario Moretti.

I couldn't say that it made me feel any better about losing Paul Applegate, but well we've been there and as we'd been told, not all outcomes would please us.

My insurance company eventually paid up for a new Pajero and I also managed a total redesign of the time travelling equipment to something much less capable of being damaged and also lighter in weight so easier to carry.

The Badgley's were completely exonerated, Joe Badgley being released from Strangeways about four months after Operation Count Your Chickens and with a small compensation package.

All the Badgley family, soon after Joe's release, moved to Ringwood in the New Forest where Stephen was able to continue with his same job working from home.

Paul Applegate and the real Malcolm Brunelli were both posthumously presented with the Kings Police Medal at their funerals.

And in early July, Samantha and I were married at Villa Comunale in Naples and having a first reception at Il Comandante and a second one at my parents place in Lyndhurst with our honeymoon spent on the Great Barrier Reef.

Most interesting perhaps was the first official day back in work at Cavendish. I'd been emailed a list of my next intake of students with their biographical profiles. There at the top of the list was a young lady named Coralie Ashton!

I was also offered a promotion. Martin Jenkins wanted to retire early as he and his wife Lucy wanted to spend some quality time together. I refused the offer knowing too well that my future lay with the CCP and with being newly married, well where I would get the time to manage a full professorship and department leader's role!

Epilogue.

Director Bedford closed the file and slid it into its outer folder. Signing the archive request sheet glued to it for its return, he put it aside to be picked up later, this time to be archived for good.

After taking a sip of his favourite cognac he sat back to reflect on those early years back in the late 2020's.

Picking up the largest of the nine framed photos he had on his desk, he sat back and smiled.

It had been a good life. Now back in 2068 he looked at the photo of his beautiful wife Samantha, their three children with their respective spouses and the seven grandchildren.

He replaced the photo in its usual place - next to a certain blue vase.

There was a knock on the door.

"Come on in." He replied.

"Simon my good man, I was just reflecting on Operation Count Your Chickens. Remember that?"

"How could I forget Director, for me it was only yesterday!"

www.ingramcontent.com/pod-product-compliance
Lightning Source LLC
Chambersburg PA
CBHW050147120726
47903CB00002B/519